I pushed open the dressing room door.

Katie looked up when Charlotte and I came in.

"I'm ready when you are," Katie told me.

Charlotte went to her locker.

"I'll be ready in a second," I said, opening my locker. "Oh, and instead of going to my house, we're going over to Charlotte's."

Katie did not look thrilled. "I don't know . . ." she said.

"Come on," I whispered to Katie. "We'll have fun."

Katie frowned. "You should have asked me before you changed our plans," she said.

Charlotte spun around to face us. "I just remembered," she said, "I'm only allowed to have one friend over at a time. Becky, you can still come."

Nobody said anything for a moment.

"Fine!" Katie yelled. "I hope you guys have fun!" She jumped up, grabbed her bag, and slammed her way out of the dressing room.

I wasn't sure what had happened. One minute, everything was cool. The [   ] as mad.

Don't miss any of the books in
this fabulous new series!

#1 Becky at the Barre

Coming soon:

#2 Jillian On Her Toes
#3 Katie's Last Class
#4 Megan's Nutcracker Prince

And look for the **PONY CAMP** series—
coming soon from HarperPaperbacks.

Becky at the Barre

Written by
Emily Costello

Illustrated by
Marcy Ramsey

HarperPaperbacks

A Division of HarperCollins*Publishers*

This is a work of fiction. The characters, incidents, and dialogues are products of the author's imagination and are not to be construed as real. Any resemblance to actual events or persons, living or dead, is entirely coincidental.

HarperPaperbacks   A Division of HarperCollinsPublishers
10 East 53rd Street, New York, N.Y. 10022

Produced by Daniel Weiss Associates, Inc.,
33 West 17th Street, New York, New York 10011.

First printing: March, 1994

Printed in the United States of America

HarperPaperbacks and colophon are trademarks of HarperCollinsPublishers

10 9 8 7 6 5 4 3 2 1

This book is for my mother, Carol Costello, and my grandmother, Hazel Keller—two women who know much of sacrifices and children's dreams.

One

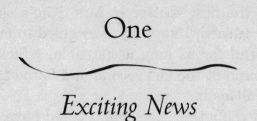

Exciting News

"You go first, Becky," someone behind me whispered.

"Don't worry," I whispered back. "I will."

My ballet class was standing in a nervous knot in the back of the studio.

"One, two, three, four," my ballet teacher, Mrs. Kim, said. She was counting in time to the music coming from the tape recorder.

I ran to the center of the studio. My feet hardly made a sound as they touched the floor. Mrs. Kim counted one, and I got ready to turn a *pirouette*. *Pirouette* means whirl in French.

Did you know that the first ballet school in the whole world was in France? It was built by King Louis XIV over three hundred years ago! That's why the names of ballet steps are in French.

Pirouettes are not hard to do. The only tricky part is not getting dizzy as you whirl around and around. That's why you have to spot.

I was the best spotter in Mrs. Kim's class. As my body turned, I kept my eyes glued to one spot on the wall for as long as possible. I flicked my head around at the last second and found the spot on the wall again.

I turned another *pirouette*. I could have turned a hundred without getting dizzy. Too bad Mrs. Kim only wanted us to do two.

"Very nice, Becky," Mrs. Kim said. "Good job!"

I ran back to my classmates with a big grin on my face.

You already know my first name. My whole name is Becky Hill. I am nine years old. I have straight penny-colored hair with bangs, and brown eyes. I also have fair skin and freckles. Everyone thinks my freckles are cute. I think they're gross.

Here are the two most important things to know about me: (1) My best friend is Katie Ruiz. (2) I want to be a ballerina when I grow up.

Becoming a ballerina is difficult. It takes years and years of practice. Even though I'm only nine, I'm already working at making my dream come true. I attend the Beginner II class at Madame Trikilnova's Classical Ballet School twice a week. I always pay attention and do my very best.

I think Madame Trikilnova's is the best ballet

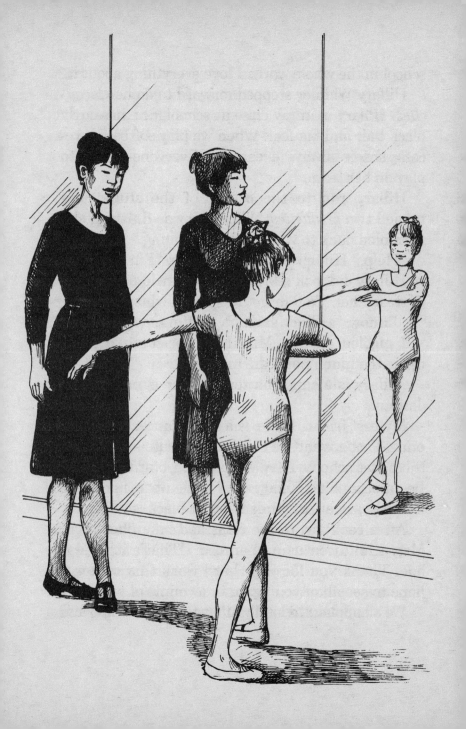

school in the whole world. I love everything about it.

Hillary Widmer stepped forward to do her *pirouettes*. Hillary is in my class at school. She has curly black hair and big feet. When we play softball at recess, she is always a captain. Everyone wants to play on her team.

Hillary ran to the center of the studio and turned two *pirouettes*. When she was finished, she stumbled back to where I was standing.

"Help," Hillary whispered to me. "I'm dizzy."

Hillary did look a little wobbly. I held out a hand to steady her. "You forgot to spot," I whispered.

"I know," Hillary said. "Now I'm *seeing* spots."

I giggled *quietly*. Mrs. Kim doesn't like us to make too much noise during class.

Hillary is a super batter, but she is not a great dancer.

My best friend, Katie, *is* a great dancer. Katie is a pink. That's what we call Intermediate students at the ballet school. They wear pink leotards to class. Beginners—like Hillary and me—wear light-blue leotards. Advanced students wear black leotards.

After each girl in the class had taken her turn, Mrs. Kim faced us and smiled. "That's it, everyone. Thank you for your hard work this winter. I hope to see all of you again in a couple of weeks."

We all applauded loudly. It's a tradition to applaud

the teacher at the end of each class. I guess it shows how much you like the person. And I liked Mrs. Kim.

After the clapping had died down, I sighed. The last ballet class in the winter session was over. I would not have class again for two whole weeks.

Hillary and I started to leave the studio.

Mrs. Kim was gathering up her tapes and the tape recorder.

"Good-bye, Mrs. Kim," Hillary yelled.

"See you in two weeks," I added.

"Bye!" Mrs. Kim called without looking up. Then she seemed to remember something. "Becky, may I talk to you?" she asked.

I shrugged. "Sure."

"You may go, Hillary," Mrs. Kim said.

Hillary and I exchanged glances. I wondered if I had done something wrong.

Hillary left, looking curious.

Mrs. Kim gave me a warm smile. "Are you planning to take ballet lessons again when the new session starts?" she asked when we were alone.

"Definitely!" I said. "I love ballet."

"You have improved a lot this winter," Mrs. Kim told me. "When you register for the spring session, I want you to sign up for a pink class, Intermediate One."

I was so excited, I could not say a word. Instead

of speaking, I jumped up and down and gave Mrs. Kim a big hug.

"Congratulations," Mrs. Kim said.

"Thanks!" I managed to get out. I ran toward the studio door and then turned around. "Thanks a lot!"

Mrs. Kim laughed. "You're welcome."

I ran into the dressing room. I couldn't wait to tell someone my terrific, terrific news. I couldn't wait to tell *everyone*. But Hillary had already gone. The dressing room was almost empty. Only a few girls from the Beginner I class were still around. Their mothers were helping them get dressed.

It was a chilly February day. But I didn't take time to change out of my sweaty dance clothes. I pulled my jeans on over my tights and leotard. I wiggled into my jacket. Then I threw the rest of my stuff into my bag and ran outside.

Katie was waiting for me on the steps of the school. See why she's my best friend? She's always there when I need her. Katie is nine, just like me. Her eyes are exactly the same color brown as mine. Other than that, we look totally different. Katie has long light-brown hair that falls in loose curls. She doesn't have bangs. She has dark freckle-free skin, and she tans super easy. When she smiles, Katie has terrific dimples.

6

"Guess what?" I said.

Katie opened her mouth to guess, but I didn't give her time to say anything.

"I'm going to be a pink!" I yelled. I started jumping up and down again. I couldn't help myself. I was very excited.

Katie was jumping up and down, too. "Wow!" she said. "That is so great."

I stopped jumping. "I just thought of something terrible," I said.

Katie stopped, too. "What?" she asked.

"The next two weeks are going to be *sooo* long," I whined. "I can't wait for my first pink class."

Katie laughed. "Don't worry. I'll keep you busy. Come on. Let's go to the coffee shop and celebrate. I'll buy you a cherry Coke."

Cherry Coke is my favorite. Of course, Katie knew that.

"All right!" I said.

Two

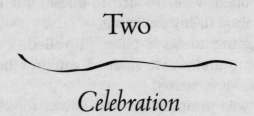

Celebration

"I win!" Katie yelled.

"You had a head start," I said, running up behind her. "I'll win next time."

"We'll see," Katie said.

Katie and I had raced from the ballet school to the coffee shop. It was a short race. That's because the coffee shop is right next door to the ballet school.

Mrs. Stellar looked up from her book when the bell on the door jingled. "Hi, Katie," she said. "How was class, Becky?"

"Great!" I said.

Mrs. Stellar has shoulder-length light-brown hair and big blue eyes. She always wears jeans, gym shoes, and a white apron. When the coffee shop isn't busy, you can usually find Mrs. Stellar reading a book. She likes super-fat books about things that happened hundreds of years ago.

Mrs. Stellar and her husband own and run the coffee shop. They know all the kids in town. That's because we kids love to hang out at the coffee shop.

Our favorite booth was empty. Katie and I slipped in on opposite sides. If any of our friends came by, there would be plenty of room for them too. We can squeeze in eight kids. Even better, our booth looks out onto Main Street. We can see everyone who walks by.

Katie and I live in Glory, Washington. Glory is such a small town that practically everyone knows practically everyone else. All the adults look out for the kids. You can't even say a bad word without someone's mom or dad *tsk tsk*ing you. That's a drag. But the parents in Glory let even little kids run around town by themselves. That's cool.

Once, Katie and I tried to figure out why the town was named Glory. We even asked Mr. Byrne and Mr. Frantz, these two ancient men who always sit on the bench in front of the bank. We figured they were probably sitting in that same spot when the name was picked. But they didn't know where the name came from. Nobody did.

Katie and I decided the town was called Glory because it's so beautiful. Glory is perched way up in the mountains. From Main Street, you can see even more mountains in the distance. Everything is green and peaceful. Glory even smells good—like rain and fir trees.

"Hello, ladies. What will it be?" That was Mr. Stellar. He had come over to our table.

Mr. Stellar has black hair and a bushy mustache. He wears the same kind of white apron as Mrs. Stellar, except his is dirtier. Mr. Stellar does most of the cooking at the coffee shop. You can tell because his apron is always covered with coffee grounds or egg yolk or spaghetti sauce.

Mr. Stellar never carries a pad and pencil when he's waiting tables. He remembers orders without writing them down. I've never seen him make a mistake once.

"A cherry Coke for Becky," Katie told Mr. Stellar. "And water for me."

I knew why Katie had ordered water—she only had enough money for one drink. Katie does things like that.

"We'll share the Coke," I offered.

Mr. Stellar brought the drink. Katie and I each put a straw into it. With our heads together, we each took a big sip.

"Congratulations!" Katie said.

"Thanks!" I said.

Katie and I have been best friends for as long as I can remember. We rode our tricycles together.

We started kindergarten at the same time. We were in the same first- and second-grade classes at Glory Elementary School.

This year, all that changed. Katie's parents decided to send her to Catholic school. I had to start third grade without my best friend. Katie and I were both bummed out all last summer. But now the school year is more than half over and it hasn't been that bad. Katie lives just two doors down from me. We see each other almost every day after school.

Katie is the person who got me interested in ballet. She's been dancing for *years*. Katie started taking movement classes when we were four. She switched to tumbling when we were five. Katie's first ballet class was the day after her seventh birthday. You have to be at least seven before Madame Trikilnova will let you into the ballet school. I remember Katie counting down the days.

Katie doesn't take movement or tumbling anymore. But she still has ballet twice a week and modern dance once a week. She takes her modern dance class at the recreation center.

I started taking ballet classes just last year. Katie called me a copycat, but I knew she was secretly happy I was studying dance.

"I can't believe we're going to be in the same ballet class," I told Katie. "It's going to be great."

"I know," Katie said. She sounded as excited as I felt. "This almost makes up for us not going to school together."

"Almost," I said.

"Your dancing must have improved tons," Katie said.

I nodded. My dancing had gotten better because I had worked hard in Mrs. Kim's class all winter. I even practiced the steps from class at home. Now my extra work was paying off. I felt wonderful.

"I'm always going to remember this day," I announced. "Even when I'm a prima ballerina."

"When you're a prima ballerina?" Katie repeated with a laugh. "Watch out, Darci Kistler! Here comes Becky Hill."

I rolled my eyes. In case you don't know, Darci Kistler is a famous ballerina. She dances for the New York City Ballet. I'm no threat to her. Katie just likes to make fun of me whenever I talk about becoming a ballerina. She says it's silly to think about becoming a professional dancer when you're only nine years old. I don't agree. What's wrong with planning ahead? What's wrong with dreaming about dancing onstage in front of an audience? It gives me goose bumps just *thinking* about it.

I didn't say all these things out loud. Katie and I have argued about this a million times already. I didn't feel like fighting. I was too happy.

"Tell me about everyone in the pink class," I demanded.

Katie took a sip of our cherry Coke. She looked thoughtful. "Well, you already know Risa, Nikki, and Megan," she said.

That was true. Risa Cumberland, Nikki Norg, and Megan Isozaki are my best friends after Katie.

Megan is in my class at Glory Elementary. Nikki is in the fourth grade at my school. Risa goes to Catholic school with Katie, but I've spent lots of time hanging out with her. We've all been to tons of slumber parties together.

"What about everyone else in the class?" I asked. "I want to know everything."

"You're definitely going to love Pat," Katie said.

Katie didn't have to tell me who Pat was. Pat was Patricia Kelly. She teaches the pink class. I had seen Pat lots of times in the halls of the ballet school. She's really pretty and nice. Katie likes her a lot.

"Did you know Pat used to dance with the Pacific Northwest Ballet?" Katie asked me. The Pacific Northwest Ballet is the company in Seattle.

I shook my head. "How come she's not dancing there anymore?" I asked.

"She broke her ankle last year," Katie said. "It's still not strong enough for her to dance on.

That's why she's teaching. I guess, when her ankle is better, she'll go back to Seattle."

"Wow," I said. "Poor Pat. She must miss performing."

Katie nodded and frowned.

I tried to be all sad and quiet out of respect for Pat's injury. But I just couldn't. "So, what else?" I demanded.

Katie laughed. "Let me think. . . . Well, Lynn Frazier is one of the nicest people in the class."

I nodded. Lynn was a fourth-grader at my school. I knew who she was, but I had never met her.

"Do you know Kim Woyczek?" Katie asked.

"I think so," I said. "Isn't she in Nikki's class at school?"

Katie nodded. "Kim's really cool, but some of the kids in the class make fun of her for being fat."

"That's mean," I said.

"I know," Katie agreed. "And Kim is only a little bit overweight."

Mrs. Stellar came up to our table. "Do you kids want anything else?" she asked.

"No, thanks," I said.

Mrs. Stellar laid our check on the table. She picked up our empty glass and headed for the kitchen.

"The Stellar twins are in the class, too," Katie

said as if she had just remembered.

Mr. and Mrs. Stellar have twin sons, Dean and Philip. The twins are the same age as Katie and me. They are fraternal twins. That means they don't look like each other. Dean and Philip are in my class at school.

"Boys! I'm going to be dancing with *boys*," I said. "That's a big change."

Katie nodded. "There are three boys in Pat's class," she said. "Dean, Philip, and John Stein. You know John's dad. He teaches advanced classes at the ballet school." Katie picked up the check and looked at it. "That's pretty much everyone."

"Don't forget about Charlotte Stype," I said.

Katie made a face. "I wish I *could* forget about her."

I giggled. "I think it's going to be great to be in her class."

Charlotte is a fourth-grader at Glory Elementary. She's tall but not too tall. She has very long, very straight blond hair. Charlotte has perfect posture. She always walks with her toes turned out. She can do a full split. Charlotte looks like a storybook ballerina.

Katie has been taking ballet with Charlotte for two years. She doesn't like her.

"I don't understand why you're excited about

being in class with *her*," Katie said.

"Simple," I said. "Charlotte is a great dancer. You're always telling me how terrific she is."

"I tell *you* how terrific she is," Katie said. "But I would never tell Charlotte. That girl is already stuck on herself."

Suddenly Katie covered her mouth with one hand and let out a squeal. "You're finally going to see Chris Adabo!" she exclaimed.

"Oh, cool," I said.

Chris Adabo is a boy Katie, Risa, Nikki, and Megan all have crushes on. He joined the advanced class at Madame Trikilnova's a few weeks ago. I think he used to go to a ballet school in Mt. Vernon. (That's a town near here.)

Since my old blue class met on Wednesdays and Saturdays, and Chris's class met on Tuesdays and Thursdays, I was never at the studio at the same time Chris was. That's why I had never seen him. But the pink class meets on the same days as Chris's class. I was sure to see him now!

I'm not boy crazy like my friends. But I was curious about Chris. Katie had just given me another reason to look forward to becoming a pink.

Three

The Red Shoes

"Hi, Sophie!" I said as I let myself in through our back door. The back door opens into the kitchen. My older sister was sitting at the table. Her homework was spread out in front of her.

"Hey, Becky," Sophie said. "Mom's already home, and dinner's ready. We were just waiting for you." Sophie stood up and gathered her books and papers together. "Set the table fast," she said. "I'm really hungry."

I could smell vegetable lasagna—Mom's specialty—bubbling away in the oven. My stomach rumbled. Dancing is hard work. I was starving.

Did I tell you about my family? No? Well, Sophie is thirteen. She started going to Glory Junior High School last fall. She's changed lots since then! Sophie used to take ballet lessons, but she claims she doesn't have time to dance anymore. *She* says she has too much homework. *I* say she's too busy chasing boys. What a waste of time! I'm never going to be too busy to dance.

I have a little sister too. Her name is Lena. Lena is only six, but she can already do a perfect *plié*. I taught her. I think Lena is going to be a great dancer someday—just like her middle sister.

My mom is a single parent. She divorced my father when I was four. Dad moved to Alaska and we haven't heard from him since. I don't miss him much. Neither does Sophie. I guess that's because Mom and Dad fought a lot when they lived together. Lena doesn't even remember Dad.

Mom has an important job at a big computer company near Glory. The company is called BPC. Mom says a full-time job is plenty of work for one woman. She says that if she also had to take care of us kids and the house, she would go crazy. That's why we have Angela.

Angela is our mother's helper. She comes over every day after school to watch Lena. If one of us older kids comes home, Angela watches us too. We're allowed to have friends over when Angela is at our house, as long as things don't get too wild.

Angela is supposed to cook and clean, too. But she usually doesn't have time. Angela says just watching Lena is enough to keep her busy.

That's why Mom needs our help, too. Sophie, Lena, and I do lots of chores around the house. Setting the table is one of my jobs.

I can set the table fast. Once, Sophie timed me with a stopwatch. I did the whole job in three minutes and twelve seconds.

I had already finished setting the table by the time Mom came into the kitchen and gave me a kiss.

"Hi, pumpkin," Mom said. "How was your day?" Mom always calls me pumpkin. Don't ask me to explain it. I think it's weird.

Mom had already changed out of her work clothes. She was wearing sweatpants. Her hair was pulled up into a ponytail. She smelled like soap.

"My day was great!" I told her. I wanted to tell her *why* it had been great. But before I could get a word out, Lena and Sophie came in.

"Hi, Becky!" Lena yelled. "Hi!"

"Hi, stinker," I greeted her.

Lena stuck her tongue out at me.

"Let's eat," Sophie said.

Mom pulled the lasagna out of the oven. Sophie grabbed the salad and salad dressing from the refrigerator. I poured milk for Sophie, Lena, and me. I got a glass of iced tea for Mom.

Everyone sat down. Mom dished up the hot food. Then we passed the salad. By the time my plate was full, I couldn't keep my news in any longer.

"I'm going to be a pink!" I announced.

Mom gave me a smile. "I'm proud of you, pumpkin."

"Wow," Sophie said. "That's great."

"Good," Lena added.

My family knew all about the pinks, but they still asked me thousands of questions. Mom wanted to know about my new teacher. Lena asked who would be in my new class. Sophie told me that Mom had thrown her old pink leotards away. They were too grubby to pass down. *That* was good news. I hate hand-me-downs.

After dinner Lena carried the dishes to the sink. I helped her with the big ones. Sophie put the leftovers away. Mom rinsed the dishes and stacked them in the dishwasher. We were just about finished when a face appeared in the back-door window.

"Hi, Katie!" Lena called.

I went over and let my friend in.

"Hello," Katie said to everyone. "I brought you a present," she added to me.

Katie held out her hand. She was holding a pink hair-ribbon.

"Thanks," I said, giving Katie a hug. "I love it."

"You can wear it to your first pink class," Katie

suggested. "It'll match your leotard."

"I will," I promised.

"I'm glad you're here," Mom told Katie as she dried her hands on a dish towel. "You can help us celebrate Becky's special day."

"Okay," Katie said. "What are we going to do?"

"Let's rent a movie," Mom suggested. She turned to me. "You can pick anything you want."

"All right!" Sophie and I shouted. We're both movie freaks.

Mom took the card for the video rental store out of her wallet. She handed it to me. Then Mom gave Sophie some money.

"What's this for?" Sophie asked.

"Ice cream," Mom said. "Sophie, make sure *you* pick the flavor."

Everyone laughed. It's no secret Mom doesn't like my taste in ice cream. She says it's too "adventurous." Mom doesn't like Rocky Road or anything with marshmallow in it. She likes fruit ice cream, so once I bought Rhubarb. Turns out, rhubarb is not a fruit. Even I have to admit rhubarb ice cream is too adventurous. Blech! It tastes like old dishwater.

Sophie, Katie, and I ran down to Main Street. Katie came into the video store with me. Sophie went on to the grocery.

I love the video store. It has rows and rows of

shelves stuffed full of different movies. There's a whole shelf of kiddie stuff Lena can watch over and over. Mom likes the old black-and-white movies on the Classics shelf. That was the direction Katie headed.

"Have you seen this?" Katie asked me. She was holding up a box for an old movie called *The Red Shoes*. "Pat told us about it in class. It's about ballet and it's supposed to be great."

"Let's get it," I said.

Katie grinned. "I was hoping you would say that."

I checked out the movie. By the time Katie and I got outside, Sophie was waiting. She was carrying a gallon of Fudge Ripple ice cream.

We ran all the way home. When we got there, Mom had already put Lena to bed.

I dished up four big bowls of ice cream.

Katie called home and got permission to stay at my house until the movie was over. Her parents said yes even though it was a weekday and she was going to be up a tiny bit past her bedtime. Katie's mom and dad are used to her spending plenty of time at my house. I spend lots of time at her house, too.

Mom, Sophie, Katie, and I settled down in front of the television in Mom's bedroom. While we watched the movie, Sophie braided my new ribbon into my hair. Then she twisted the braid into a bun. It looked great.

In case you're thinking about renting *The Red Shoes,* you should know the ending is super sad. By the time the last images flashed across the screen, I was crying.

Katie rolled her eyes at me. "It's only a movie," she said.

"But it was so sad," I said.

Sophie stood up. "I'm going to bed," she told us with a big yawn.

"Good night," Mom, Katie, and I said.

"Good night," Sophie answered.

"Okay, you little ballerinas," Mom said. "It's time for you to hit the sack, too. Come on, Katie. I'll walk you home."

Katie jumped up. "I'm still glad you're going to be a pink," she told me, "even though movies make you act like a freak."

"Thanks," I said with a sniffle.

"I forgot to tell you about my great idea!" Katie suddenly exclaimed. "That's why I came over here in the first place."

"What?" I asked.

Mom yawned. "Make it quick," she said.

"My mom is planning a party for Alison's kinder-garten class," Katie said. Alison is Katie's little sister. She's five and a half. "I thought we could invite all our friends over the same day and have our own party in honor of you becoming a pink."

"That sounds great," I said.

"It also sounds like a lot of work for your mother," Mom told Katie. "You'd better ask for her permission before you start making plans."

"I already asked," Katie said. "Mom and Dad said it was cool."

"Don't worry," I told my mom. "I'm going to help. I'll do at least half the work."

"Speaking of work," Mom said. "I have to get up early in the morning. Come on, Katie. Let's get you home."

Mom and Katie headed for the back door. I went upstairs and crawled into bed. I couldn't believe Katie was giving me a party. Then again, prima ballerinas are probably treated this way every day of their lives.

Four

New Tights and Leotards

"Come on, Mrs. Ruiz," I mumbled to myself that Saturday. "Hurry up and get here."

Me and my mom, Katie and her mom, Risa, Nikki, and Megan were all going shopping in Seattle. Katie's mom, Mrs. Ruiz, had offered to drive. The Ruizes have a big van.

I was ready and waiting on our front porch even though Mrs. Ruiz wasn't supposed to pick us up for another fifteen minutes. I only get to go to Seattle once in a while. I couldn't wait to get going.

Seattle is about thirty miles from Glory. Remember how I told you Glory is in the mountains? To get to Seattle, you have to get to the bottom of those mountains. Seattle is on the water. It's a big city full of people, cars, and boats. I like to go to Seattle because the best dance store around is there.

When Mrs. Ruiz finally pulled up in front of

our house, I yanked opened our front door.

"Mom!" I yelled.

"Coming!" she yelled back.

I ran down our walk and got into the middle seat of the van with Katie.

Mrs. Ruiz turned around and smiled at me. "Hi, Becky," she said. "I'm happy to hear you're going to be a pink. Are you looking forward to the party?"

"Yes!" I said with a big grin. "Thanks for letting us have it."

"No problem," Mrs. Ruiz said. "It's going to be fun."

I spend so much time at Katie's, Mrs. Ruiz is practically my second mother. She looks a lot like Katie. She has the same brown eyes and curly hair. But Mrs. Ruiz's hair is cut short.

Mom came out of the house and got into the front seat.

Lena and Sophie waved good-bye to us from our front porch. Sophie was going to baby-sit Lena while we were in Seattle. Sophie just started baby-sitting a few months ago. Mom pays her. Isn't that cool?

We all waved good-bye to my sisters as Mrs. Ruiz drove down the street. She picked up Megan next.

"Hi," Megan said as she climbed into the van.

"Hi," we all chorused back.

Megan's dad is Japanese and her mom is Irish.

27

She looks a little like each of them. Megan has long hair with curly wisps near her face. Her hair is brownish-black with a lot of gold and red highlights in it. Megan's skin is a pretty warm color. She has hazel eyes and is super skinny.

Mrs. Ruiz turned down Main Street. Nikki and Risa were waiting in front of Nikki's apartment building.

Nikki is all hair. When you look at her, you see a mass of light-brown curls that reaches the middle of her back. Nikki is the only one of my friends with pierced ears. That day she had on a pair of butterfly earrings covered in glitter.

Risa is African-American. She has beautiful green eyes. Her hair isn't that long, and she wears it in a bushy ponytail on top of her head. On school days Risa has to wear a geeky uniform. (So does Katie.) On all other days Risa wears great clothes. She'd chosen purple high-tops and a sweatshirt with rainbow stripes for our trip to Seattle.

"Way to go," Risa greeted me as she crawled into the van.

"Thanks," I said.

It had been three days since I'd gotten my good news. Nikki and Megan knew all about how I was going to be a pink. I talked about it during lunch every day at school.

I hadn't seen Risa in over a week, but Katie had told her the news while they were eating lunch at *their* school.

"Are you excited?" Risa asked.

"Of course!" I said. "I can't wait."

Mom turned around in her seat. "Aren't you going to miss the kids in your old class?" she asked me. "And what about Mrs. Kim? You always loved her."

"I guess I'll miss Mrs. Kim," I admitted. "And Hillary. But, Mom, pink class is much better than blue class."

"Why?" Mom asked.

"In the blue class, we had to use a tape recorder," I said. "Pinks get a piano player. Blues dance in the basement. Pinks dance in a pretty studio on the second floor."

"Besides," Katie put in, "I'm a pink. And so are Nikki, Risa, and Megan."

"Right," I said. "Also, pinks get to wear pink leotards and tights."

"What's so great about that?" Nikki asked.

"Pink is my favorite color," I told her.

Katie gave me a funny look. "Since when?"

I wrinkled my nose. "I guess, just since last Wednesday," I admitted. "Before that, purple was my favorite color."

Everyone laughed.

When we got to Seattle, Katie's mom parked in front of the Capezio Dance–Theater Shop. Capezio's is a big store packed full of dance stuff. I love the place.

Mrs. Ruiz and Mom got a table in a coffeehouse down the street from the store. They never go inside with us. We take too long and it drives them nuts. This way they can read the newspaper and chat while we shop.

Mom had promised to buy me a new pink leotard and two pairs of pink tights. She gave me the money. My friends and I ran down the street and into the store.

"Come over here," Nikki said. "I want to show you something." She led us toward a display of posters.

"Wow," I breathed.

"It's a new section," Nikki explained. "I saw it last time I was here."

Posters of famous dancers and dance companies filled the wall. More were rolled up and stored in bins. There were posters of all kinds of dancers—modern, jazz, tap, even flamenco. We all crowded around.

Megan sighed. "Jock Soto is so cute."

Jock Soto dances for the New York City Ballet. He's a total hunk. Besides the poster of him, there were others of Darci Kistler, Heather Watts, Suzanne Farrell, and more. From the Pacific Northwest Ballet, there were posters of Patricia Barker, Susan Gladstone, and Steven Annegarn.

"I'm saving money to buy this poster of Patricia Barker," I announced. The poster was incredible. Patricia Barker was dancing in *Swan Lake*. The photographer had caught her in the middle of a *grand jeté*. That's a kind of jump. Her arms and legs were flung wide.

My friends came over to study the poster.

"Her feet have a great arch," Megan said.

"Her arms are beautiful," Risa added.

"Come on," Katie said. "Let's look at the leotards."

Katie led the way over to the leotard display. There were tons of leotards: long-sleeved, short-sleeved, crossovers, and ones with crisscrossed straps. It took us at least an hour to sort through all of them. There was so much to choose from! I couldn't decide. Finally Katie talked me into buying a short-sleeved leotard. That was the kind she had, and she wanted us to match.

I paid for the leotard and two pairs of pink tights. The saleswoman put all of my stuff in a Capezio bag. She stapled the top together.

Next we headed to the shoe department. Nikki had to buy a new pair of ballet slippers. Her feet had grown a whole size since she had gotten her last pair. While the saleswoman measured Nikki's foot, the rest of us wandered around.

"Look," Risa said. "Toe shoes."

Megan, Katie, and I went over to examine the shoes Risa was holding.

Toe shoes look a lot like regular ballet slippers, but they're covered in a shiny fabric and have satiny ribbons that you have to sew on. The toes of the shoes are different in an important way. They're hard.

I don't know exactly how toe shoes are made. I asked Mrs. Kim once. She told me the people who make them keep their methods a big secret. All I know is that the shoes are made by hand and they cost a lot.

"I can't wait to go on pointe," I told my friends.

Dancing on pointe means dancing on your toes. Most girls don't go on pointe until they're about twelve. You have to have super-strong feet, ankles, and legs. Boys hardly ever dance on pointe.

"We're going to look beautiful," Megan said.

Risa nodded. "Like we're flying."

Katie examined the toe shoes. "We're going to get megablisters," she said.

The rest of us groaned.

"Thanks a lot, Katie," I said.

Katie grinned. She likes to tease us when we

get starry-eyed about dancing.

Nikki joined us. She was carrying a Capezio bag just like mine.

"I'm finished," Nikki announced.

Katie looked at her watch and let out a little scream. "We've been in here forever," she said. "We'd better get going before my mom freaks."

Risa, Katie, Nikki, Megan, and I hurried toward the exit.

As we were walking out the door, a woman was walking in. She looked familiar, but I didn't think I had ever met her. It took me a minute to figure out who she was.

"Hey, you guys," I whispered. "Look! That's Patricia Barker."

My friends all turned around to look.

"It *is* her," Risa agreed.

"So?" Nikki asked. "What are you going to do? Ask for her autograph?"

I grinned. "Good idea."

"Really?" Megan's eyes were wide.

"Definitely," I said. "Come on!"

My friends shook their heads.

"No way," Megan said.

"I'll wait here," Risa added.

"Chickens," I said to them. I ran after the woman by myself. "Ms. Barker!" I yelled.

The woman turned around and gave me a questioning look.

Wow, I thought. *It really is her.* Suddenly my tongue was frozen to the roof of my mouth. I was about to chicken out when someone poked me in the back.

It was Katie. "Go on," she said. "Ask her."

"I, um . . . we were wondering," I managed to say. "Would you sign this?" I held out my Capezio bag.

Ms. Barker smiled and took my bag. She fished around in her purse. "Sorry," she said. "I don't have a pen. Do you?"

Katie and I shook our heads. My heart sank. I wasn't going to get the autograph after all.

"Do you mind if I use eyebrow pencil?" Ms. Barker asked.

Katie and I shook our heads again.

"What are your names?" Ms. Barker asked.

"I'm Becky," I said, beginning to relax. "And this is my best friend, Katie."

Ms. Barker wrote something and handed the bag back.

"Thank you," Katie and I said together.

"No problem," Ms. Barker said. She seemed amused.

Katie and I said good-bye to her and ran back to our friends.

"Did you get it?" Megan asked.

"Yes!" I exclaimed. I showed everyone the bag. It read, "To Becky and Katie: Never stop dancing. Best friends are forever. Yours, Patricia Barker."

"That's so cool," Risa said.

"I want one," Nikki said. "Becky, will you get Patricia Barker's autograph for me?"

"No way!" I said.

"Let's go," Megan said.

We ran outside and down the street.

When Mom saw us, she looked at her watch. "You've been gone for more than two hours," she announced.

"We're sorry," I said.

"Don't be," Mrs. Ruiz said with a laugh. "I think you just set a new record. You've never gotten out of Capezio's faster!"

Five

The Big Day Arrives

I opened my eyes and jumped out of bed. I ran to my window and peeked out. It was a sunshiny morning.

"Yes!" I whispered to myself.

The day of my first pink class had finally arrived. It had been a long wait. Our shopping trip in Seattle had been on a Saturday ten whole days earlier. Ten days may not sound like a long time to you, but it felt like an eternity to me. Now I just had to make it through one more school day, and it would be time for my first pink class.

I was humming as I walked down the hall to the bathroom.

Sophie was just coming out. "What are you doing up so early?" she asked. "Wait, don't tell me! You're too excited about your ballet class to sleep."

"Right," I said. "How come you're up so early?"

"I have a big history test today," Sophie said with a grown-up sigh. "I guess I'm too nervous to sleep. Hey, since we both have extra time, do you want me to do your hair before school?"

"Would you?" I asked. "Cool!"

I washed up and got dressed as quickly as possible. Then I got out the pink ribbon Katie had given me. Sophie braided the ribbon into my hair and then put the braid up in a bun, just like she had the evening we watched *The Red Shoes*.

I twisted around and tried to see my bun in the mirror. I couldn't. Sophie held a hand mirror up behind my head. I could see the reflection from the hand mirror in the big mirror in front of me.

"I look beautiful," I announced. "Thanks, Sophie."

"Do you want some lipstick?" Sophie offered. "Or how about some eyeliner?"

"No way!" I said. The last time I let Sophie give me a makeover, she used much too much makeup. When she was done with me, I looked like a monster from the ballet *The Firebird*.

"Okay," Sophie said with a laugh. "Then, get lost. I have to decide what to wear to school."

I rolled my eyes. "Big decision!" I said. "Let me know if you need help."

Sophie threw a notebook at me as I dashed for her bedroom door. I went back to my room and grabbed my dance bag. My new pink ballet clothes were already inside.

I ran downstairs and made my lunch. I made Lena's lunch too. That's another one of my chores. Then I kissed Mom good-bye, grabbed an apple for breakfast, and headed for Megan's house. Megan and I walk to school together.

"Hi, Becky," Megan said as she came out of her house. "Are you excited about your first pink class?"

"Yes," I said. "I'm also nervous."

"Nervous?" Megan asked.

"What if I'm not good enough?" I blurted out. "What if Pat sends me back to the blue class?"

"Don't worry," Megan told me. "Pat is super nice. She would never do that."

I already knew Katie liked Pat. But it was nice to hear that Megan liked her, too. Those ten days of waiting had given me plenty of time to think of all kinds of disasters that could happen in my first pink class. I was worried about everything from getting a hole in my tights to breaking both my legs.

When Megan and I arrived at Glory Elementary School, the bell was ringing. My class was lining up on the playground to go inside the building. Megan and I ran to get in line.

I like school. The third grade is especially cool. My teacher, Mr. Cosgrove, tells great stories. He takes us on lots of field trips, too. Mr. Cosgrove has shaggy blond hair and a brown beard. He would be perfect if he didn't give so much homework.

I've known almost all of the kids in my class for years. One girl was new, though. Her name is Jillian Kormach. She moved to Glory this winter.

The Intermediate I dancers in Mr. Cosgrove's class are Megan Isozaki, Dean Stellar, and Philip Stellar. Hillary Widmer is in the class, too. And now me!

Dean and Philip got into line behind me and Megan.

"Hi, Meg," Dean said.

"Hi," Megan whispered. She's super shy around boys.

Like I said before, Dean and Philip are fraternal twins. It's easy to tell them apart because they don't look anything like each other.

Philip has dark-brown hair and brown eyes. He is short and sturdy-looking. Philip always wears a Seahawks cap backward. The Seahawks are the professional football team in Seattle. Mr. Cosgrove even lets Philip wear his cap in the classroom. I think Mr. Cosgrove must be a Seahawks fan, too.

Dean is taller and thinner than his twin. His hair is brown, too, but much lighter and curlier. His eyes are blue.

"Hey, you guys," I said to the twins. "I'm so excited about ballet class this afternoon. Aren't you?"

"Keep it down," Philip said. "I never talk about—"

"Hey, Philip," Mark Miller called in a high-pitched voice. "I hope you didn't forget your tutu." Mark is totally gross. He picks his nose during class. He always plays dodgeball at recess. I hate dodgeball.

"Thanks a lot, Becky," Philip said. "That was just perfect." He stomped toward the back of the line. I could tell he couldn't wait to get away from me.

I felt my face get hot. "I only—I'm sorry," I told Dean.

"Don't worry," Dean said. "Phil is kind of uptight about ballet."

"Becky is nervous about her first pink class," Megan told Dean.

"You'll be fine," Dean said to me. "Just remember to watch out for Al."

"Al?" I asked.

"The piano player," Megan explained.

"What's wrong with Al?" I asked. Katie had never said anything about watching out for Al.

Megan giggled. "Usually he's fine," she said. "But once in a while . . ."

"Watch out," Dean put in. "Weird alert!"

Megan giggled again.

I was surprised Dean was still talking to us about ballet class. He didn't look embarrassed or worried that the other boys were going to tease him. He seemed to like ballet a lot. There hadn't been any boys in my blue class. I wasn't sure how I felt about dancing with them. I tried to imagine Philip doing a *grand plié*. That made me smile.

We walked into the classroom. Dean headed for his seat. Megan and I headed toward our seats. Megan sits on one side of me. That vulgar Mark Miller sits on the other side.

"Wouldn't it be funny if Dean and Philip wore pink leotards to class?" I whispered to Megan as Mr. Cosgrove took attendance.

"I can't believe you said that," Megan said, giving me a *look*.

In case you don't know, boys always wear the same thing to ballet class. No matter what level they're in, they wear a white T-shirt, black tights, white socks, and black ballet slippers. But thinking about having boys in my class made me imagine Dean and Philip dressed in pink leotards. I wanted Megan to think about it, too. I thought it would make her laugh.

Megan was not laughing. She was frowning.

"I was just joking," I said to defend myself.

"It's not funny," Megan said. "You're always

41

talking about how great Baryshnikov is. How do you think he learned?"

Baryshnikov is my favorite male ballet dancer in the whole world.

"He must have gone to a lot of classes to get so good," I admitted.

"So, what's wrong with Dean and Philip being in our class?" Megan wanted to know.

"Nothing, I guess," I said. "Sorry."

The truth was, I felt funny about having boys in my class. After all, Philip and Dean are not Baryshnikov.

I wondered why Megan was acting so fierce. Why would she want to stick up for the twins?

Six

New Girl

"Do you like Charlotte Stype?" I asked Nikki at lunchtime.

Nikki reached over, grabbed one of my peanut-butter crackers, and started to eat it. "Not really," she mumbled. Crumbs flew out of her mouth.

"Nikki, that is so gross," Megan complained.

Nikki stuck her tongue out at Megan. It was covered with half-chewed crackers.

I laughed.

Megan rolled her eyes.

Nikki and Megan and I eat lunch together every day. We all pack our lunches and share whatever we bring. It's more interesting that way.

"Katie doesn't like Charlotte at all," I told Nikki. "But she's in your class at school. You know her a lot better than Katie does."

"Charlotte is a little strange," Nikki said. "Just

this morning Mrs. Edwards had to try and get Charlotte's attention three times."

Mrs. Edwards was Nikki and Charlotte's teacher.

"She kept saying Charlotte's name," Nikki said. "But Charlotte didn't even look up. So Mrs. Edwards walked over to Charlotte's desk and picked up the paper she was scribbling on. It was covered with little drawings of toe shoes." Nikki shook her head. "The girl never thinks about anything but ballet."

I glanced over to where Charlotte was sitting with Lynn Frazier. I didn't see anything wrong with spending a lot of time thinking about ballet. I spent a lot of *my* time thinking about ballet, too.

"Charlotte sure seems popular," I said.

Lots of kids were gathered around Charlotte. Almost all the fourth-graders in the lunchroom stopped by her table to say hi.

"Charlotte isn't popular," Nikki said. "Lynn is."

I watched the other table more closely. It was true. Charlotte was eating without saying much. Lynn was laughing and talking to everyone.

"I don't like Charlotte, either," Megan spoke up. "She always acts like she's the best dancer in our class."

I shrugged. "Katie told me she was," I said.

44

"Maybe she is," Megan admitted. "But she doesn't have to *act* like it."

I took a sip of my milk. None of my friends liked Charlotte, but their reasons seemed silly to me. I wondered if they were jealous of her.

While I was thinking about Charlotte, Jillian Kormach pulled a chair up to our table. I was surprised. Jillian had never eaten lunch with us before. Like I said, she had just moved to Glory. She had been in Mr. Cosgrove's class only a few weeks.

Jillian is African-American. She has light skin and long hair that falls in incredible soft curls.

"Hi," Jillian said. She looked uncomfortable.

"Hi!" Megan said in a super-friendly voice.

Jillian started Glory Elementary at a hard time. The school year was already more than half over. It was kind of late to make new friends. None of the girls in Mr. Cosgrove's class, including me and Megan, had paid much attention to her. "Nikki, this is Jillian," I said. "She's in Mr. Cosgrove's class with me and Megan. She just moved to Glory from New York City."

"New York?" Nikki repeated. "That's so cool! How come your family moved to Glory?"

"My grandparents live here," Jillian explained.

"You must be so mad at your parents," Nikki said. "If I lived in New York, I'd never want to leave. Besides, moving is the pits. Last year my family moved down the street from where we used to live. I was totally bummed out."

Nikki paused to breathe. Then she hurried on. "I can't even imagine moving all the way across the country. You'll probably never see your friends in New York again."

"Yes, I will," Jillian said. "My dad still lives there. I'm going to visit him twice a year."

"Did your parents get divorced?" Nikki asked.

Jillian nodded. "A few months ago," she whispered.

Nikki was about to ask another question, but Megan gave her a look. Nikki closed her mouth fast.

Nikki is a very curious person. Some people say she's nosy. She upsets people with her questions. That's not because Nikki is cruel. It's because she doesn't notice when she's making people uncomfortable.

Megan doesn't like to see people upset. That doesn't mean she never expresses her opinion. But it does mean she always thinks before she speaks. Nikki never does.

"My mom and dad are divorced, too," I told Jillian. I didn't want her to feel like she was the only one whose parents had split up.

Jillian didn't say anything for a minute. She just sat there, looking sad.

"Oops," Nikki mouthed silently to me and Megan.

Megan and I shook our heads at her.

Jillian broke the silence. "I heard you guys talking to Dean this morning," she said. "I dance, too. My mom called the ballet school here yesterday. The woman there—she had a strange name. . . ."

"Madame Trikilnova," I said.

"Right," Jillian said. "Madame Trikilnova told my mom I should come by the school this afternoon."

"Maybe you're going to be in our class," Megan said.

"That would be neat," Nikki added. "Then we'd have two new people."

"I'm becoming a pink today," I explained to Jillian. "That's what we call intermediate dancers. We wear pink leotards."

"I hope I'm in class with you guys," Jillian said. "It's more fun to dance with kids your own age. Besides, I already have a pink leotard. I even brought it with me today."

"You might have to start as a blue, though," Nikki told Jillian. "That's what we call beginners. But don't worry. There are lots of third-graders in that class, too."

47

Jillian shook her head. "I'm not a beginner," she said. "I've had a lot of training. I probably belong in the advanced class. I studied at the School of American Ballet for a whole year."

Megan, Nikki, and I exchanged looks. The School of American Ballet is one of the best ballet schools in the country.

"I can't believe you were in an advanced class at the School of American Ballet," I said. "That's incredible!"

"Hold on," Jillian said with a laugh. "I wasn't in an advanced class in New York."

"Then what makes you think you'll be in an advanced class here?" Nikki asked.

"Nikki," Megan spoke up. "Jillian's probably way ahead of us."

"Yeah," I agreed. "After all, the School of American Ballet is really famous, and our school is—"

"Just a small school in a tiny town," Jillian finished for me.

That wasn't exactly what I had been about to say, but I nodded. Jillian was right. Compared to the School of American Ballet, Madame Trikilnova's is small. Compared to New York City, Glory is tiny.

Nikki looked offended. She crossed her arms and turned away from Jillian. She pretended to be very interested in something going on across the lunchroom.

"Peter Martins visited my class in New York once," Jillian said.

"Wow," Megan said.

"That's so cool," I added. I wasn't exactly sure who Peter Martins was, but I guessed he was a famous dancer.

"You'll be in the advanced class," Megan told Jillian.

Nikki spun around to face Jillian again. "I'm so jealous!" she said as if she couldn't help herself. "The cutest guy in Glory is in that class. His name is Christopher Adabo. He's a seventh-grader and he has—"

"The most incredible eyelashes," Megan put in.

"And green eyes," Nikki added.

"There will be boys in my class?" Jillian said. "That's a relief!"

"Weren't there boys in your class in New York?" I asked.

"Sure," Jillian said. "But things are different in the City. Glory is so small. I thought people might act backward about boys and ballet."

Megan smiled at me. I knew she was thinking of my joke about the twins' wearing pink leotards. I stuck my tongue out at her.

"Do you want to walk over to the ballet

school with us later?" Megan asked Jillian.

"Okay," Jillian agreed.

Nikki gave Megan a funny look. "Great idea," she said. She rolled her eyes so that only I could see. It was clear that Nikki didn't like Jillian.

I shifted in my seat. I thought Jillian was okay, but I didn't want to walk with them. I knew it would take them forever to get there.

"I can't go with you," I said, thinking fast. "I have to hurry. I, um . . . I have to give Madame Trikilnova my check for the new session."

This was a lie. Mom always drops off the check herself. I tend to lose things. Mom says I can't be trusted with anything important. I couldn't help lying. I wanted to get to class early.

"The rest of us can still go together," Megan said.

Nikki and Jillian nodded. The three of them made plans to meet on the front steps after last period. A few minutes later the bell rang and lunch was over.

In class that afternoon, I looked at the clock at least a million times. It was moving so slowly, I was sure it was broken.

When the final bell finally rang, I was out of my seat in a flash.

Jillian and Megan were still gathering up their books when I took off running toward the ballet school as fast as I could.

Seven

My Favorite Place

I ran down Main Street. I passed the library, the video store, the post office, the grocery, and the hardware store. I waved at Mr. Stellar as I passed the coffee shop.

A few steps more and I reached my favorite place in the whole wide world.

My favorite place is a low red brick building. The wooden front door is painted sky-blue. A brass sign reads: MADAME TRIKILNOVA'S CLASSICAL BALLET SCHOOL.

I pushed open the heavy front door. Inside, the building was hushed. Soft foot-thumping came from Studio D on the second floor, where the advanced students were warming up.

I stepped inside. The door slammed shut behind me. The loud noise made my heart skip a beat.

Madame Trikilnova poked her head out of her office and frowned at me.

I smiled back at her.

Madame Trikilnova always looks ready to dance. She wears a black leotard and a flowing black skirt every day. Her long blond hair is forever pinned up in a tight bun. She's very thin and stands very straight.

"What is all this noise?" Madame Trikilnova demanded. "And what are you doing here? Your class does not begin for almost an hour."

"I—I know," I stammered. "I wanted to make sure I was on time."

Madame Trikilnova stepped out of her office. She put on her glasses—which she wears on a gold chain around her neck—and studied my face.

I felt like a bug under glass. Madame Trikilnova makes me nervous. Everyone I know is afraid of her. Even my mother! (Madame Trikilnova told Mom to hush at my recital last year.)

Madame Trikilnova is very strict. Maybe that's because she's Russian. She trained at the famous Vaganova School of the Kirov Ballet. When she was younger, she danced all over the world—in Moscow, Paris, London, and New York.

I reached up and tried to fix my bangs. They were sticking to my forehead. I knew my face was bright red. It gets that way when I'm hot.

"It looks like you ran all the way from school," Madame Trikilnova commented.

"I did," I admitted.

"I see," Madame Trikilnova said. "I understand you are joining the pinks today."

"Yes," I said. I couldn't stop myself from grinning.

"It's exciting for you, no?" Madame Trikilnova asked.

"I'm a little nervous," I admitted. Why did I have to keep telling everyone that?

Madame Trikilnova smiled. "Just work hard, and you will do fine. Now, go ahead and get changed. I'll unlock the studio for you. You can stretch out while you wait for the others."

"Thanks a lot!" I told Madame Trikilnova.

She waved me off and stepped back inside her office.

I rushed toward the dressing room. What I saw on the way there surprised me so much, I stopped dead. The waiting area was empty! I had *never* seen it empty before.

On days when the blue classes meet, the waiting room is full of parents. Parents brushing their daughters' hair. Parents gossiping with each other. Parents reading books to little kids. Parents doing everything parents do.

Madame Trikilnova has a rule: No parents may

observe classes without her permission. She never gives permission. Madame Trikilnova says having people peek into the studio distracts the dancers. All the parents who bring their kids to ballet have to hang out in the waiting area.

But it was Tuesday. No blue classes met on Tuesdays. Intermediate and advanced students clearly didn't need their mommies and daddies to come to ballet with them. That empty waiting area made me feel very grown-up.

I hurried into the dressing room and threw my bag down on a bench.

Giselle stood up and yawned with her entire body.

"Having a stretch, old girl?" I asked, giving her a rub behind the ears. "That's what I'm about to do, too."

Giselle is an orange-and-white tiger-striped cat who has adopted the ballet school. She doesn't really belong to anyone, but all the teachers feed her. Madame Trikilnova pretends to think Giselle is a nuisance, but we know she loves her.

Giselle sleeps on an old sweater on top of the lockers. Once in a while she comes to class and watches us dance. She doesn't need Madame Trikilnova's permission like the parents do.

I yanked off my school clothes and pulled on my

tights and leotard. I walked over to the mirror and admired my new dance clothes. I looked great!

I put a T-shirt and a pair of white leg warmers on over my leotard and tights. I always wear extra layers at the beginning of class. I take them off when I get warmed up.

As soon as I was dressed, I ran upstairs. The hallway on the second floor was empty. Madame Trikilnova had disappeared. Except for the muffled sounds coming from Studio D, everything was quiet.

Studio C was unlocked. I stepped inside and let out a happy sigh. This was much nicer than being stuck in the basement with the blue class.

Studio C is beautiful. Two wooden handrails— one higher than the other—run around three walls of the studio. The rails are called barres. There are two so that people of different heights can pick the one that's right for them. Above the barres are big windows. On sunny days, light floods the room.

The fourth wall of the studio is covered with a mirror from floor to ceiling. The floor is made of wood.

Near the door is a box of rosin. Rosin is cool stuff. If you rub the soles of your ballet slippers in it, they grip the floor better.

In one corner of the studio is a ratty upright piano.

I went to the barre and began stretching out. . . .

It was opening night at the Opera House in Seattle. A spotlight shone down on me. I danced the last steps of the Sugarplum Fairy's solo in *The Nutcracker.* The audience broke into thundering applause. The crowd was on their feet. Someone handed me a huge bouquet of roses. I took a deep curtsy—

"What do you think you're doing?"

I snapped out of my daydream. Charlotte Stype was standing in front of me. She looked furious.

"Wh—what's the matter?" I asked.

"You're standing at *my* place at the barre," Charlotte told me. "You have exactly three seconds to move!"

Eight

A New Friend

I stared at Charlotte. Her arms were crossed and her face was red. She was staring back at me.

"I'm sorry," I said, feeling awful. "I didn't mean to—to do anything wrong."

Charlotte didn't move. She didn't say a word.

"My name is Becky Hill," I said to fill up the silence. "I go to Glory Elementary with you. I'm in the fourth grade."

Charlotte just kept staring at me.

"This is my first day as a pink," I went on. "That's why I didn't know this was your spot. I'm really excited to be in your class. Everyone says you're a great dancer. I bet I can learn a lot from you."

Charlotte cleared her throat. She tapped her foot.

Suddenly I realized what was wrong. I still hadn't moved out of her spot. I stepped away from the barre.

Charlotte took her hands off her hips.

"Here," I said. "Why don't you take this spot now? You must want to stretch out before class."

Charlotte put her left foot up on the barre. She leaned over and touched it with her right hand.

"Listen," I said. "I really am sorry."

"Don't worry about it," Charlotte said. "It's not a big deal, I guess."

"Great," I said. I wanted to get away from Charlotte. I was beginning to see why my friends didn't like her. "Have a good class—" I started to say.

"I like this spot at the barre because Pat can see me best from here," Charlotte said. "That's important if you want your technique to be perfect."

"I think good technique is so important," I told Charlotte.

"It is," Charlotte said. "That's why the best dancers always stand in front."

Nikki and Megan came into the studio. I was hoping they would rescue me, but they just shot me surprised looks. They picked spots at the barre as far away from Charlotte and me as possible and started to stretch out.

Lynn Frazier came in next. I was relieved when she walked toward us. Lynn was eating lunch with Charlotte that day at school, remember? I found out later that Charlotte and Lynn are best friends.

Lynn is African-American. She has dark skin and dark eyes. She wears her hair in long cornrows pulled up into a ponytail. She's very pretty.

"Hi, Charlotte," Lynn said. She smiled at me.

"This is Becky," Charlotte told Lynn.

"I'm Lynn," Lynn told me. "You go to Glory Elementary, don't you?"

I nodded. "I'm in the third grade."

"You'd better stretch out," Charlotte said to me. "Take that spot," she said, pointing to a place at the barre next to her.

"Well . . ." I said hesitantly. I guessed that was where Lynn usually stood.

Lynn seemed to read my mind. "Go ahead," she said. "There's lots of room. I'll just move down a little."

I stepped into the space between Lynn and Charlotte. I did a few *demi-pliés*. (That's ballet language for "half knee-bends.") Mrs. Kim says *demi-pliés* are the best way to warm up your legs.

Risa came in and walked over to Megan and Nikki.

"What's Becky doing?" I heard her ask.

"Shh!" Megan said.

My friends' voices died down. I knew they were whispering about me. I fought the urge to turn around.

Al, the pianist, arrived next. He is very thin and pale. He has a big mop of messy brown hair. He was wearing tennis shoes and carrying a bicycle helmet. One pant leg was taped down. I guessed Al rode his bike to class.

Al scowled at us, sat down, and started playing scales. He seemed a little grumpy but not as odd as I expected, considering what Megan and Dean had said. I decided to keep an eye on him just in case.

By the time Katie arrived, the studio was full of kids. She hurried up to me, still pulling her hair into a ponytail.

"What are you doing up here?" Katie asked. "Don't you want to stand with me and Nikki and Risa and Megan?"

I turned pink. Katie was making me look silly in front of Charlotte and Lynn.

"No, thanks," I told her. "I want to be up front, where Pat can see me."

"How come?" Katie asked. "You'll have more fun if you stand next to us."

"I don't want to have fun," I said. "I want to work on my technique."

"Oh," Katie said, sounding confused.

I turned back to my stretches. I was imitating the leg exercises Charlotte was doing.

"I guess there isn't any room for me up here,"

Katie said, glancing at Lynn and Charlotte. She was trying to give them a hint, but neither one of them offered to move.

"I guess not," I told her.

Megan waved at me and Katie. "I saved room," she called. Megan had saved enough space for two people. I knew one spot was for me, but I didn't want to get stuck way back where my friends were standing. Pat probably wouldn't be able to see me there at all.

"I guess I'll see you later," Katie said uncertainly.

"Okay," I agreed.

Katie walked back toward our friends. I knew I hadn't been nice to her, but I was still happy to be up front with Charlotte and Lynn. Charlotte said the best dancers always stand in the front. I wanted to be one of the best.

Nine

My First Pink Class

Th-umph. Th-umph. Th-umph.

That was the sound my heart was making as the time for class to start got closer.

I watched the other kids doing exercises and talking with their friends.

Nikki was trying to fix her hair.

The boys were all standing together. Dean was doing toe touches. Philip was talking to John Stein. I was pretty sure John was in the fourth grade at Glory Elementary.

While I was watching the boys, the studio suddenly quieted down. Pat had come in.

Pat is beautiful. She has shiny black hair, fair skin, and a few pretty freckles across her nose. (Not all over her face, like me.) Pat has a nice smile. She was wearing a black leotard, pink tights, and shiny shoes with a heel.

"Hi, everyone," Pat said.

"Hi!" the class yelled back.

Pat glanced down at her class list. "I know most of you from last session," she said. "But I would like to welcome two new students to our class."

I looked around. I was wondering who was new besides me. I noticed that some of the other kids looked confused, too.

Pat turned to me. "Are you Jillian?"

"No," I said. "My name is Becky Hill."

"Sorry," Pat said. She looked down at her list and made a mark with a pencil. "Here's your name."

Just then the studio door opened. Everyone turned to see who was coming in. It was Jillian, of course. She told Pat her name and then took the place right in front of Katie.

I wondered what Nikki and Megan thought of Jillian joining our class. I guessed Nikki was not too happy.

Pat clapped her hands. "Okay, everyone," she said. "Let's get warmed up. We'll see how well you all remember the barre routine. Becky and Jillian, do your best to follow along. I'll help you."

Charlotte was standing in front of me. She put her left hand on the barre. I put my left hand on the barre. I relaxed while I waited for Pat to turn on the tape recorder.

I had forgotten about Al. I jumped when he started to play. While I tried to figure out what was going on, the rest of the class moved into a *demi-plié*. It was two seconds into my first class and I was already behind!

Quickly I glanced down and saw that Charlotte's heels were together and her toes were pointed outward. That's first position.

I put my feet in first and dropped into a *demi-plié*. By then everyone else was standing up straight.

Pat came and stood beside me.

I felt a little panicked.

"Your arm is in front, to the side, *plié*, and up," Pat said in time to the music.

Arms? I had forgotten all about my arms.

"Front, side, *plié*, up," Pat said again.

I concentrated on Pat's words. Soon I fell in step with the others. Pat walked toward the back of the class.

I took a deep breath and tried to relax.

"Good," Pat said. "Now *en seconde*."

I was lost. Then I noticed Charlotte had moved her feet farther apart. I remembered that *en seconde* is French for second position. By the time I got my feet into the correct position, I was behind again.

I was working too hard following the exercises to pay much attention to what my classmates were doing. Still, I couldn't miss the noise Katie, Risa, and Nikki were making by whispering and giggling.

I was surprised. I talk in class all the time. But only when I'm not dancing. When I *am* dancing, I concentrate on dancing.

"And more of the same," Pat said. "*En cinquième.*" That means fifth position.

I brought my right heel against the big toe of my other foot. Then I did the routine. I was starting to feel like I was finally catching on when Pat said, "*Relevé* and turn."

Before she had gotten the words out, everyone in class rose up on the balls of their feet (*relevé* means to rise) and turned to face the other direction. Now their right hands were on the barre. I turned half a beat after the rest of the class.

I was looking at Lynn's back. Charlotte was behind me. I could feel her eyes on *my* back. I didn't want to make any more mistakes. I willed myself to dance perfectly.

"Jillian, follow your arm," Pat said. "That's it. Much better. Megan, that looks beautiful."

I liked Pat already. She didn't make you feel stupid when you made a mistake. And even though I did my best, I made lots more mistakes during the barre exercises that day. I couldn't help but let Charlotte see I wasn't perfect.

The problem was that everyone else in the class knew the barre routine. They didn't need to watch Pat when she demonstrated each of the exercises. But I had to. And even so, it was hard to remember everything. I had to follow Lynn's and Charlotte's movements. This meant I was always a step behind.

I was relieved when we finally left the barre to do center work.

"Are you having fun?" Katie asked me as the class took their positions.

"It's hard not knowing the exercises," I said. "But I'm having fun anyway. I can't believe class is already half over."

"Come on," Katie said. "Risa is saving us a place."

"I want to stand up front," I said. "Come up there with me."

Katie wrinkled her nose. "I never stand in front," she said. "Besides, Risa is waiting for us."

Pat clapped her hands. "Take your places!" she said. "Let's get started."

"I want to stand where Pat can see me," I insisted.

"Fine," Katie said, sounding angry. "See you later." She went to stand with Risa, Megan, and Nikki.

I squeezed into the first row. Charlotte and Lynn were already at the center of the front line. Charlotte gave me a big grin as I joined them.

Center work is a lot like the barre. We repeated many of the same exercises. But this time they were harder because we didn't have the barre to hold on to.

"Good job," Pat told us after the center work. "You can move back now."

My favorite part of class had arrived! We were going to do traveling steps or jumps, or maybe even both. I hoped there would be time for both.

The class gathered in a back corner of the studio. Pat stood in the opposite front corner of the room, facing us.

"I want you to do four *grand jetés* across the studio," Pat told us. *Grand jetés* are a kind of jump. "Take three running steps between each one to get yourself started. Try to use up the whole floor. When you land, I want you to be able to touch my hand. I'm not moving from this spot."

The other students nodded their heads. I guessed Pat had asked them to do this exercise before.

"This is simple," I whispered to Charlotte.

"Just wait," she whispered back.

Al began playing some happy music.

Lynn went first. She leaned forward and gave Pat a high five when she finished. Her *grand jetés* looked fine to me. But not to Pat.

"Good stretches," Pat told Lynn. "But you were

half a beat ahead of the music. And don't forget to point your toes."

Katie crossed the floor next. Pat had to reach way out to touch her hand.

"You need a bigger stretch," Pat told Katie. "And don't forget to think about what your arms are doing."

I smiled at Charlotte. I understood what she had meant. Pat was very picky.

Jillian went next. Her *grand jetés* only covered three-quarters of the floor. Pat couldn't even come close to touching her hand.

"You need to come down into a *demi-plié*," Pat told Jillian. "That will help you land softly. Try to spring up a bit higher. And don't forget to think about stretching out as far as you can."

Megan, Nikki, and I exchanged glances. Jillian's jumps did not look good. I could see Megan was as surprised as I felt. Nikki was smiling. She seemed happy Jillian wasn't dancing well.

Charlotte went next. She easily shook Pat's hand when she landed.

"Beautiful," Pat told her. "Good work."

I was next in line, but I stepped back. I didn't want to go after Charlotte. Neither did anyone else. I wasn't used to feeling unsure in ballet class. In Mrs. Kim's class I had always volunteered to go first.

"Come on," Pat said. "Becky, I think you're next."

I stepped forward. I was nervous, but I tried to concentrate. I didn't do a very good job. My jumps felt off. I knew they weren't pretty. When I landed, Pat took a giant step forward and shook my hand.

"Good try," Pat told me. "You're just a little tensed up."

I frowned. "Can I go again?" I asked. "I know I can do better."

"Let's give everyone else a chance first," Pat said. "You can try again if we have time."

We did not have time.

"Okay, that's it," Pat said as soon as the last person took her turn. "We're running late. See you on Thursday."

All of the kids applauded Pat and Al. Then they all started to file out of the studio.

"Hurry up, Becky," Katie called.

"Coming," I said, but I didn't follow her.

I didn't want to leave the studio until I got my second turn.

Al slipped into his jacket.

Someone told Pat she had a phone call, so she hurried out of the studio.

Al came and stood in front of me. He looked me right in the eye and frowned as if he was deep in thought.

"Hi," I said nervously.

"You're going to make it," Al declared.

"What?" I asked.

Al didn't answer. He tucked his music under his arm and left.

I shrugged and walked over to the corner of the studio. Everyone had gone. Now that nobody was watching me, I could concentrate.

"One, two, three," I whispered to myself as I ran. Then I jumped.

Ten

Katie Left Behind

I landed with a big smile on my face. This time my jumps had felt just right. I even ended up close to where Pat had been standing.

"Good job, Becky," I told myself, doing my best to imitate Pat's voice.

I threw my fist into the air. "Yes!" I exclaimed.

"That was much better," I heard someone say.

I spun around.

Charlotte was standing in the door of the studio.

I felt my face grow hot. Why was Charlotte spying on me? Why had I been acting like such a freak?

"I'm sorry if I surprised you," Charlotte said with a little smile. "I came back to look for you. Do you want to practice some more?"

"I guess I need to," I said. I didn't tell Charlotte, but I didn't like being the worst dancer in class.

"Why don't you come over to my house?"

Charlotte suggested. "We can practice together."

I was surprised by the invitation. Charlotte was the best dancer in Intermediate I. All my friends had been telling me how mean she was. I couldn't believe she was being so nice.

"Thanks," I said. "That sounds like fun. I just need to get my stuff out of my locker."

Charlotte smiled. "I'm ready to go. I'll wait for you in the waiting area."

"Okay," I agreed. "I'll be right out."

I hurried into the dressing room. My friends were standing in a circle, whispering about something.

I rushed over to my locker and opened it.

Katie looked up. "Where have you been?" she asked me.

"In the studio," I told her.

"Can you believe Jillian is in our class?" Nikki asked.

"Nikki," I said, glancing over my shoulder.

Katie guessed what I was thinking. "Don't worry," she said. "Jillian already left."

"I was surprised," I told Nikki. I started to pull off my leotard. Then I realized I wasn't finished dancing for the day. I slipped my arm back inside.

Nikki turned to Risa and Katie. "At school today Jillian made it sound like she was ready to solo for the Pacific Northwest Ballet."

"We were positive Madame Trikilnova would put her in an advanced class," Megan said.

"So was Jillian!" Nikki added.

I had pulled on my jeans and tennis shoes. I put on my jacket. Then I threw everything else in my bag and slammed my locker shut.

"See you later," I called to the others as I headed for the door.

"Where are you going?" Katie asked. "We're going to hang around until the black class gets out. Then we can walk home together."

"Well, I—" I started.

"You have to stay," Nikki said. "This is your big chance to check out Chris Adabo."

"I can't believe you're finally going to see him," Katie said with a grin.

Risa picked up her bag. "I'm ready," she said.

"Come on," Megan said. "Let's wait in the hall."

"I can't stay," I said.

"How come?" Katie asked. "You have lots of time before dinner."

"I'm going to Charlotte's," I said.

Katie looked shocked. "Charlotte's? Why are you going there?"

"Charlotte asked me to, that's why," I said, getting a little huffy. "Is there something wrong with that?"

"I thought you wanted to see Chris," Katie said.

"I do," I told her. "But I can see him any day we have class. Charlotte is going to help me practice."

"What about the party?" Katie said. "We still have to plan things."

"We have plenty of time," I said. "The party isn't for almost two weeks."

"When did you and Charlotte Stype get to be such good friends?" Nikki asked me.

Risa and Megan stood behind her, frowning.

"We aren't good friends," I said with a sigh. "We're just going to practice together."

Katie shrugged. "Have fun."

"Are you mad at me?" I asked.

"No," Katie said.

I didn't believe her, but I didn't have time to talk about it just then. Charlotte was waiting. I decided to worry about Katie and the others later.

Eleven

Charlotte's Studio

"What took so long?" Charlotte demanded.

She was waiting for me on the couch in the waiting area. Madame Trikilnova keeps a little table there full of programs of ballets she's seen. There are also copies of *Dance Magazine*. I can sit there and read for hours without getting bored, but Charlotte looked impatient. She threw down the magazine she was reading as soon as she saw me.

"I'm sorry," I said. "We were talking about Jillian in the dressing room."

"What about her?" Charlotte asked as she pushed open the door to the street.

"She just moved here from New York City," I said. "Today at school she told us she took classes at the School of American Ballet." I was about to ask Charlotte if she knew about the school, but I didn't have to.

"She's so lucky," Charlotte said with a faraway smile. "Think of all the famous dancers she must know. I wonder if she ever met Peter Martins."

"She said he came to her class once!" I exclaimed. "But, uh . . . who's Peter Martins anyway?"

"He's the director of the New York City Ballet," Charlotte told me. "He doesn't perform anymore, but he was a great dancer. He's a choreographer too." A choreographer is a person who creates dances.

I was impressed Charlotte knew so much about Peter Martins. Not many kids in Glory know more about ballet than I do, and I hadn't even known who he was.

"It must be great to take classes in New York," I said.

Charlotte nodded. "I would love it. But Jillian didn't learn much. She doesn't dance very well."

"Her jumps weren't that great today," I agreed. "But maybe she was just nervous. It was her first class at the school."

Charlotte shrugged. "Good dancers don't let how they feel affect their performance."

I didn't say anything to that. I had been nervous in class that afternoon and it had affected *my* performance.

"This is my house," Charlotte said after we had walked about six blocks.

We turned up the footpath in front of a big white house with shutters. A volleyball net was set up in the front yard. A bunch of teenage boys were playing.

"Hi, squirt!" one of the boys yelled.

"Wanna dance?" another one called.

Charlotte ignored them.

"Who are they?" I asked.

"My stupid brothers and their dumb friends," she told me. "Just try to pretend they don't exist."

Charlotte opened the front door and led me inside. She introduced me to her mother, who was reading a magazine in the living room. Then we went upstairs to Charlotte's room.

Charlotte flopped down on her bed, which had a big canopy and a pink bedspread. The room was not exactly neat. (Mine isn't, either.) Copies of *Dance Magazine* were thrown all over the floor.

I turned in a circle at the center of the room.

The walls were covered with posters of dancers—Amanda McKerrow, Darci Kistler, Heather Watts, Baryshnikov, and more. "This is cool," I told Charlotte.

"Thanks," Charlotte said. "I've been collecting ballet stuff forever."

I walked closer to the wall to examine a poster advertising the Pacific Northwest Ballet's staging of *The Nutcracker*.

The Pacific Northwest Ballet's version of *The Nutcracker* is famous. Maurice Sendak designed the sets and costumes. He's the man who wrote and illustrated *Where the Wild Things Are* and lots of other children's books. *Where the Wild Things Are* is one of Lena's favorite books. My family goes to see *The Nutcracker* every year.

"I want to show you something," Charlotte said. She jumped up and opened her desk drawer. She pulled out a bunch of brochures and handed them to me. They were from ballet schools all over the country.

"How did you get these?" I asked.

"I sent away for them," Charlotte said. "My mom helped me. I have to pick one pretty soon. I'm going away to a professional ballet school as soon as I'm old enough to audition."

I looked at the brochures more carefully. There was one from the Pacific Northwest Ballet School in Seattle. There were also brochures from New York City, San Francisco, Los Angeles, Washington, D.C., and even some place in Massachusetts.

"Would you really move away from home?" I asked.

"Sure," Charlotte said. "That's what you have to do if you want to become a professional dancer. But I can't even try out for a couple of years. Most of the schools make you wait until you're at least twelve."

"If you went to the school in Seattle you could still live at home," I said.

"I don't care about that," Charlotte told me. "I'll go to the best school I get into no matter where it is."

"Do you want to be a ballerina?" I asked.

"More than anything in the world," Charlotte said.

"Me too," I whispered.

I thought about how Katie always teased me for wanting to be a ballerina. She made me feel like it was an impossible dream. Charlotte made it seem possible. Still, I wasn't sure I would be brave enough to move away from home in a couple of years. I would miss my family and Katie and Madame Trikilnova's ballet school.

"Come on," Charlotte said, jumping up again. "I have something else to show you."

Charlotte led me downstairs into the Stypes' basement. She opened a door with a sign that read KEEP OUT posted on it.

"I call this my studio," Charlotte told me. She stepped inside and turned on a light.

Charlotte's studio was a rec room with a wall of mirrored panels.

"I moved all the furniture away from the wall," Charlotte told me. "I use this chair as a barre."

Charlotte walked over to a sturdy desk chair that stood in front of the mirrors. She placed her hand on the back of the chair and from first position slowly raised her right leg way up in front of her. Charlotte had incredible extension. She had perfect control of her leg. It didn't even shake.

"This is great," I told Charlotte. "I dance at home sometimes, too. But I don't have a mirror to use."

"I'll get another chair for you," Charlotte offered. "Then we can practice the barre exercises from class."

"Okay," I agreed.

Charlotte pulled a chair in from another room in the basement. She dragged it up to hers.

"We'll start with some *demi-pliés*," Charlotte said.

I had done thousands of *demi-pliés* before that afternoon. I thought I didn't even have to think about them anymore.

Charlotte did not agree. She watched my *demi-pliés* with a frown.

"Look at your hand," Charlotte told me. "It's too relaxed. You're letting it flop down from the wrist."

I did a few more *demi-pliés*. I concentrated on making my hand look more graceful.

"Your hand is better," Charlotte told me, "but you're standing up too quickly. You should take the same amount of time to straighten your legs as you did to bend them."

Charlotte was an even tougher teacher than Pat. She made me do *demi-pliés* until they were perfect. Then Charlotte suggested we move on to *grand pliés*. When I could do those perfectly, we practiced every other exercise in Pat's barre routine.

Charlotte gave me lots of advice. By the time her mother called her for dinner, I felt much more comfortable with Pat's barre. I was also more impressed than ever with Charlotte's dancing ability.

"Thanks a lot for your help," I told her. "You really are the best dancer I know."

"You're welcome," Charlotte said. "You're a good dancer, too. You learn fast."

I felt great as I walked home. My first pink class had been harder than I thought it would be, but Pat had not sent me back to the blue class. And after all of Charlotte's help, I was positive I would do much better on Thursday.

I had also made a new friend. I thought Charlotte was super nice. I planned to tell Katie about all the help she had given me. Maybe then Katie would start to like Charlotte as much as I did. I decided to talk to Katie the very next afternoon.

Twelve

Getting Better

Things don't always turn out the way you plan. I didn't have a chance to talk to Katie about Charlotte the next afternoon or any day that whole week. I got very busy all of a sudden.

On Wednesday Mr. Cosgrove assigned my class a book report. We could read any novel we wanted. The librarian at school suggested I read *Little Women* by Louisa May Alcott. She said it was a classic and that she had loved it when she was my age. The school library didn't have any ballet books for kids my age, so I checked it out.

Little Women is a fat book. I spent hours lying on the living room couch, reading it. I spent hours sitting at the kitchen table, reading it. I spent hours curled up on my bed, reading it. After all that I still had a lot of pages left to read.

On Sunday I finally finished reading *Little Women*.

I still had to write up what I thought of it. I didn't see what the librarian liked about it. The only good character was Jo. The other girls in the book were always fainting and blushing and mending socks and dreaming about getting married. Blech!

I spent all of my free time at Charlotte's practicing. Charlotte and I went over Pat's barre hundreds of times. I learned it backward and forward. Charlotte and I worked on my center work and jumps, too. I had never practiced ballet as much. It was fun. I could feel myself improving. I started to look forward to class even more.

Usually I see Katie every day. That week I only saw her in ballet class. I *saw* Katie, but I stood with Charlotte and Lynn. Katie got to class just before Pat did. She stood with Megan, Risa, and Nikki. Katie left as soon as class was over. We never had time to talk.

By the end of the week I had about a hundred things saved up to tell Katie. I figured she must have been busy, too. She hadn't come over to my house once all week.

By my fourth class I had learned the routine in Studio C. This is what always happened before class got started:

Charlotte, Lynn, and I always came early. The place at the barre between Lynn and Charlotte had become my spot. The three of us stretched out while the other kids wandered in.

Megan and Risa were the next to arrive. Then Jillian and most of the others.

Al would hurry in and start banging out scales.

Katie and Nikki were always the last two to arrive. They liked to hang out in the dressing room until a minute before class started.

Seconds after Katie and Nikki got settled, Pat would come in and yell hello to everyone. She would take attendance and we would begin the barre routine.

I learned another thing those first two weeks: Pat is a terrific teacher. She's patient with everyone. She never yells or rolls her eyes. Even more important to me, Pat teaches traveling steps every class. Ms. Kim hardly ever did them.

"Okay, everyone," Pat said on Thursday near the end of class. "Move back!"

We all scrambled toward the back of the studio. I was grinning. "Move back" is what Pat always says when it's time to start traveling steps. My favorite part of class had arrived!

"We're going to do the *pas de bourrée* combination we learned last session," Pat said. *Pas de bourrée* is the name of a traveling step.

Pat walked through the short combination. Jillian

and I paid close attention. Everyone else already knew the steps. Jillian asked Pat to walk through the combination a second time. She looked worried.

I wasn't worried. I learn combinations quickly. I was happy because the combination included a *pirouette*.

Charlotte had turned to face the mirror. She was practicing her *pirouettes*.

"This is great," I whispered to Lynn. "I love *pirouettes*."

"That's because you're good at them," Lynn whispered back. "You're happy because you have a chance to show off."

I could feel my face turn red. But Lynn was smiling. I had to admit she was right. I do love *pirouettes*, and it's because I'm good at doing them.

Katie came to stand beside me. *"Pirouettes,"* she whispered. "Your favorite."

"I guess it's obvious," I said with a giggle. "Hey, what are you doing after class?"

Katie shrugged. "Homework, I guess."

"Come over to my house," I suggested.

Katie smiled. "All right," she said. "Great!"

Pat clapped her hands. "Line up in groups of three," she said. "Let's go."

Megan, Jillian, and Lynn moved across the floor first.

I watched them dance, and I noticed something that shocked me.

Jillian's *pirouettes* were wobbly. That was no surprise. But Megan kept losing her balance. Not only that—Lynn hurried through the steps and got ahead of the music.

The other pinks weren't perfect!

I don't know how I could have missed it before. It was as if someone had turned on a lightbulb.

Katie, Risa, and Nikki went next.

Katie's turnout was not turned out. Risa had to work to keep from falling over her own feet. Nikki acted silly. She made funny faces as she danced.

What a relief! For the first time I knew I was good enough to be a pink. With a big smile on my face I watched the next group cross the floor.

Philip hardly even tried. Dean tried hard and danced well. Still, his steps were a little heavy.

Kim needed more confidence. She got halfway through the combination and quit even though she was doing it right. I wondered if Kim was self-conscious because of her weight. Katie said she got teased a lot.

I lined up with John and Charlotte. I was a little disappointed I wasn't going to get to see what mistakes they made. But then I realized I had already discovered a problem with Charlotte. She never watched the rest of us dance. She preferred to watch herself in the mirror. Sometimes she didn't even pay attention to Pat.

It's bad not to watch your classmates dance. You can learn a lot from what they do right—and what they do wrong. I reminded myself that Charlotte didn't *need* to pay attention. She was already the best dancer in the class.

"Good job," Pat told me after I had finished the combination. "Your posture is improving and your spotting is great."

That was the first time Pat had praised me. I felt like a true pink. I was never going to worry about being sent back to the blue class again.

I grinned at Katie.

She gave me a thumbs-up.

I was still glowing with happiness when class ended.

"Thanks, Charlotte," I told her.

"What for?" Charlotte asked.

"For all of your help," I explained. "I'm only dancing better because of you."

Charlotte smiled. "You have improved since I started helping you," she agreed. "But don't forget that you have a long way to go."

Suddenly I felt a tiny bit less happy. But I had to admit Charlotte was right.

Thirteen

Three's a Crowd

"Do you want to come over?" I asked Charlotte as we walked toward the dressing room.

"Sure," Charlotte agreed.

"I already invited Katie," I added quickly.

I crossed my fingers and hoped Charlotte wouldn't change her mind about coming. I wanted Katie and Charlotte to get to know each other better. I thought that once they spent some time together, Katie would like Charlotte as much as I did.

"Whatever," Charlotte said with a shrug.

We passed Nikki and her mom in the hallway. Mrs. Norg had cornered Pat. She was asking all sorts of questions about recitals and performances that were still months away.

I smiled at Nikki. She looked as if she wanted to die.

Mrs. Norg is really into seeing Nikki on stage.

Nikki's ballet lessons were Mrs. Norg's idea. Nikki thinks her mother is a big embarrassment. She *is* kind of weird.

"I just had an idea," Charlotte said. "Let's go to my house instead. It'll be more fun because we'll be able to dance."

"Sounds good," I agreed. "Maybe you can help Katie with her turnout."

"It needs work," Charlotte mumbled.

I pushed open the dressing room door.

Inside, Katie was sitting alone on a bench, reading a textbook. Risa and Megan must have gone home straight from the studio. (Sometimes we put our street clothes into our bags and bring them to class. That way we can leave fast.)

Katie looked up when Charlotte and I came in.

"I'm ready when you are," Katie told me.

Charlotte went to her locker.

Katie shot Charlotte a funny look. She seemed to be wondering why Charlotte was hanging around.

"I'll be ready in a second," I said, opening my locker. "Oh, and instead of going to my house, we're going over to Charlotte's."

I hoped Katie wouldn't freak out at that news.

Katie did not look thrilled. "I don't know . . ." she said.

I glanced toward Charlotte's back. She could

hear every word we were saying.

"Come on," I whispered to Katie. "We'll have fun."

Katie frowned. "You should have asked me before you changed our plans," she said.

"What does it matter?" I said.

"It matters because the party is the day after tomorrow," Katie said angrily. "So far you haven't done one thing to help me."

Charlotte spun around to face us. "I just remembered," she said, "I'm only allowed to have one friend over at a time. Becky, you can still come."

Nobody said anything for a moment.

"Fine!" Katie yelled. "I hope you guys have fun!" She jumped up, grabbed her bag, and slammed her way out of the dressing room.

I wasn't sure what had happened. One minute, everything was cool. The next minute, everyone was mad.

"So, are you coming over or what?" Charlotte asked me.

"I'd better not," I said.

"You can come over later if you change your mind," Charlotte said.

"Okay," I agreed.

I threw the rest of my stuff in my bag, slammed my locker shut, ran down the hall and out the front door. I caught up with Katie on the sidewalk. She was walking toward her house. She was also crying.

I was surprised. I couldn't remember the last time I had seen Katie cry.

"What's wrong?" I asked, hurrying to keep up.

"Charlotte is so mean!" Katie said.

"But if her parents have a rule—" I started.

"She made that up!" Katie screamed. She stopped walking and turned to face me. "I can't believe you're sticking up for her. Didn't you see how mean she was to me?"

"Charlotte was kind of mean just now," I admitted. "But you weren't very nice, either. Charlotte could tell you didn't want to go to her house. Don't you think you might have hurt her feelings?"

"I couldn't have hurt her feelings," Katie yelled, rushing down the sidewalk. "She doesn't have any!"

"Come on," I said. "That's not true. Charlotte's nice. I think the only reason a lot of people don't like her is because she's the best dancer in class."

Katie took a deep breath. "Becky, I think Charlotte only likes you because you keep saying how great she is."

"That's not true!" I yelled. "Charlotte and I have lots in common. We have fun together."

"I bet you always do what she wants," Katie said.

"Then you don't know anything!" I said.

"You're just saying mean things because . . . because you're jealous!"

We were almost in front of Katie's house. Katie ran ahead of me, up the path, and onto her front porch.

"I am not jealous!" Katie yelled. She ran inside before I could answer. The door slammed behind her.

I stomped the rest of the way home. I was mad, mad, mad. Katie can be a big pain sometimes.

But by the time I woke up on Friday, I had cooled down. I never stay mad long.

That night Mom took us out for pizza and a movie. We didn't get home until almost bedtime. There was no message from Katie on the answering machine. I had a hard time getting to sleep.

The party was the next day. I hoped Katie wasn't still mad at me.

On Saturday I got up early and dressed in my nicest jeans and T-shirt. I couldn't wait to make up with Katie. I wanted to get working on the party. Considering that I hadn't done anything yet to help, I figured Katie and I would have a lot of work to do.

Still, I knew I couldn't just go over to the Ruizes'. Katie and I have had hundreds of fights. Katie has a terrible temper. I've learned to stay away from her until she chills out. Sometimes it takes a minute, sometimes it takes an hour. When we were six, I threw Katie's favorite doll into the ocean and it took her two whole days to forgive me.

I knew I had to wait for Katie to come over. I hate to wait. But I reminded myself that the party was in a few hours. Katie would have to come over soon. I wouldn't have to wait long.

I ran downstairs.

"Morning, pumpkin," Mom said. "You look pretty."

"Good morning," I said. "Thanks."

Mom was sitting at the table, drinking a cup of coffee and eating a piece of toast. Even though it was Saturday, Mom was going into the office. She said she had some paperwork she wanted to get off her desk. Sophie was going to baby-sit Lena.

Usually I hate it when Mom works on Saturdays. This time I was glad. I didn't want Mom hanging around, worrying about me and Katie.

Mom finished her breakfast, told me to have fun at the party, gave me a kiss, and left.

I peeked out the back door. No Katie.

Sophie and Lena woke up. I helped Sophie pour cereal and orange juice for the three of us. We ate.

No Katie.

I did the dishes even though it was Sophie's turn.

No Katie.

I got out my books and did all my homework for the weekend.

No Katie.

I watched Saturday-morning cartoons with Lena until I was bored.

No Katie.

I watched Saturday-morning cartoons with Lena until *she* was bored.

Still no Katie.

I was getting mad. It was almost noon. What was going on? I went outside and stood on the back porch. I thought I could hear voices coming from the Ruizes' house. I definitely heard music. Were my friends at Katie's? How could they be having a party in my honor without *me*?

Why hadn't Katie come?

Tears welled up in my eyes. I knew the answer. Katie hadn't come because she wasn't coming. She didn't want to be my friend anymore. Who could blame her? She was throwing a party for me, and I had been too busy with Charlotte to help.

The doorbell rang. I didn't get it. I didn't want anyone to see me crying.

A minute later Sophie opened the back door. "Katie's here," she told me.

Suddenly I wasn't sad anymore. I was angry.

"What does she want?" I asked.

"She said she had to talk to you," Sophie said.

Katie expected me to talk to her after she had tortured me all morning? No way!

"I don't want to talk to her," I said. "Tell her to go away."

"What about the party?" Sophie asked. "Katie went to a lot of trouble. The least you could do is go."

"I'm not going," I insisted.

"So what am I going to tell Katie?" Sophie asked.

"Tell her I have more important things to do," I said. "No, wait! Tell her I'm not here. Say I went to Charlotte's."

Sophie shook her head. "Why would I tell her that?"

"Because that's where I'm going!" I yelled.

Sophie went back to the front door and spoke to Katie. I couldn't hear what she said, but Katie went away.

I stomped up to my room and changed into my dance clothes. I ran to Charlotte's as fast as I could, covering my ears the whole way. I didn't want to hear my friends having fun without me.

Fourteen

No Beginner

"Errg," Nikki groaned. "That hurts!"

Risa, Megan, and I exchanged glances and giggled.

Nikki was standing over a sink in the dressing room at the ballet school. She had a brush in one hand. With the other hand she splashed water onto her hair. Nikki tried to pull her hair into a ponytail, but big pieces kept escaping.

"Go ahead and laugh," Nikki said. "You guys have normal hair. You don't understand what I go through."

On most days Nikki doesn't even try to comb her crazy hair. She just lets it go wild. It looks great that way. But for ballet class we all have to wear our hair up. That's so Pat can see the lines of our necks. Making a bun is a struggle for Nikki.

Risa walked over to the mirror and made a big show of checking her own perfect bun.

Nikki stuck her tongue out at her.

I smiled at Risa and Nikki, but I felt impatient. It was way past the time I usually went into the studio. I was hanging out in the dressing room, waiting for Katie.

None of my friends had said anything about the party. I was too embarrassed to ask what had happened.

"I just got my allowance," Megan announced. "Let's go to the coffee shop after class."

"Great," Nikki agreed. "I deserve a sundae after this."

"Becky, will you come?" Megan asked.

Before I could say anything, Katie answered for me. "Don't waste your breath inviting Becky," she said. "She's too busy playing ballerina with Charlotte to do anything with us."

I spun around in surprise. I hadn't even heard Katie come in.

My hands tightened into fists. I wanted to go to the coffee shop. I didn't have any plans with Charlotte. But I was too angry to admit that.

"Katie's right!" I yelled. "I'm going to Charlotte's house after class because Charlotte is my friend. Unlike *some* people."

Megan stepped forward. "Come on, you guys—" she started.

I didn't hang around to hear what Megan had

to say. I took my bag with my stuff inside and pushed by her. I stomped all the way to the studio.

"You're late," Charlotte greeted me.

"I know," I said. I went to stand next to her at the barre and bent forward into a deep stretch. "Katie is a such a big baby," I added as I straightened up.

"No joke," Charlotte agreed. "Listen, do you want to come over this afternoon? We can practice our *battements frappés*. And, if Pat teaches us something neat in class, we can practice that too."

I grinned. "Great!"

"Hi, you guys." That was Lynn. She had just come over from the other side of the studio. She had been talking to Kim.

"Hi, Lynn," Charlotte said. "Becky's coming over this afternoon, too."

Lynn grinned at me. "Great!"

I smiled back. Lynn is super nice. She likes everyone.

For a minute I was happy to be spending the afternoon with Lynn and Charlotte. Then I thought of something. Charlotte had told Katie she could only have one friend over at a time. But she had invited both me and Lynn over that afternoon.

Katie was right.

Charlotte had lied.

All during the barre and center work I thought

about what to do. Should I tell Charlotte I knew she had lied? She would just get mad. I didn't want Charlotte to be mad at me. One angry friend was enough. And what if Charlotte hadn't been lying? What if her parents had changed the rule all of a sudden? Stranger things have happened. I decided not to say anything to Charlotte.

"Becky, are you paying attention?" Pat asked.

"Yes!" I said.

I forced myself to stop thinking about Charlotte. I made myself pay attention to what Pat was saying.

"I'm going to teach you a new jump," Pat told the class. "They're a kind of *changement* called *royales*. Start with your feet in fifth position."

Pat demonstrated as she spoke. Most kids just watched. Charlotte and Lynn and I imitated Pat's movements.

"Your right foot is in front," Pat went on. "You bend down into a *demi-plié*. Then you jump up."

I glanced at Katie. She looked sad. Did that mean she wanted to make up? I didn't care. I didn't want to make up with her after what she had said in the dressing room.

"While you're in the air, open your legs a little," Pat went on. "Close them quickly, so that your calves hit together. Now change the position of your legs. When you land, you should be back in fifth position. But your left foot should be in front."

Pat demonstrated the jump several times, until everyone understood how it was supposed to look.

"Okay," Pat told us. "Pair up and practice. John, you're Lynn's partner. Megan, dance with Dean. Nikki and Philip, you two work together."

Whenever we work with partners, Pat makes sure the boys dance with one of us girls. That means she has to assign the boys partners. She lets the rest of us pair up however we want.

"Do you want to be my partner?" Charlotte asked me.

"Sure," I said without looking at her.

I was busy watching Megan and Nikki with the boys. I felt sorry for my friends. I would be embarrassed to dance with a boy, even a nice one like Dean. So far I had been lucky. Pat hadn't paired me up with any of them.

Megan looked miserable. And poor Nikki. She had to dance with Philip. Double disgusting! He was a boy *and* he couldn't dance.

I also noticed that Risa and Katie were partners. Katie was whispering something in Risa's ear. I wondered if it was about me.

"Earth to Becky," Charlotte said. "Are we going to practice?"

"Sorry," I said.

"You go first," Charlotte told me.

I did a several *royales* without any problem. They felt natural to me.

"Those looked good," Charlotte told me. "I guess we're not going to need to practice these at my house. They're easy."

Charlotte did a few *royales* as she spoke. "Since we can both do these, maybe Pat will let us practice something else now."

"Wait," I told Charlotte. "You're landing with your feet too far apart." I did another *royale*. "See? Your feet should look like this when you land."

Charlotte stared at me.

"What's wrong?" I asked. "Don't you understand the jump?"

"Of course I understand the jump," Charlotte said. Her voice was a whisper. "What I don't understand is who you think you are." She shook her head. "I refuse to believe that *you* are telling *me* how to dance."

"What do you mean?" I asked.

"You're nothing but a beginner," Charlotte told me. "Don't ever forget that. And don't you ever say that something is wrong with my dancing again."

"I'm sorry," I choked out. But I wasn't really. I did not like the way Charlotte was acting. I was *not* a beginner. I was a pink just like Charlotte. She didn't have any right to act like she was better than me.

Fifteen

Charlotte Is Jealous

"Okay, gang," Pat yelled. "Simmer down!"

The class had been getting loud, but Charlotte and I were not making any of the noise. We hadn't exchanged a word since Charlotte had called me a beginner. I was afraid that if I said anything, it would be mean.

"All right, everyone, let me see how your *royales* are coming," Pat said.

The class fell into lines facing front. I was in the first row with Charlotte and Lynn, as usual.

Al began to play.

Pat walked around the class as we started to jump.

"Nikki, keep your chin tucked in," Pat said. "Everyone, your arms should be down in front. I see lots of sloppy arms." Pat wandered back toward the front of the class and stopped in front of me. I concentrated extra hard.

"Becky's *royales* are perfect," Pat announced. "Why don't you come up here and show everyone?" she asked me.

I couldn't help but smile. Pat had picked my *royales* over everyone else's. I took a few steps forward. I could see everyone's reflection in the mirror.

Megan, Risa, Lynn, and Nikki were all smiling at me.

Katie's eyes were focused on a spot just above my head.

I met Charlotte's gaze and smiled at her. She didn't smile back.

Al began to play.

I started my *royales*. Charlotte leaned over and whispered something to Lynn.

"Give Becky your attention please, Charlotte," Pat said. "Your *royales* need work."

Lynn and Charlotte stopped whispering.

Charlotte was turning red.

I did a few more jumps.

"Thanks, Becky," Pat said. "That's enough."

"That was fun," I whispered to Charlotte when I was back in my place.

Charlotte did not answer.

After class Lynn and Charlotte left the studio together. I grabbed my bag and ran after them.

"Hey, you guys!" I called. "Wait for me!"

Lynn stopped and turned around. Charlotte tried to keep walking, but Lynn pulled on her arm.

I stopped in front of them. "What's up?" I asked Charlotte. "Did you forget I was coming over?"

"No, I didn't forget," Charlotte said. "I—I just remembered my parents are having a dinner party this evening. I can't have you over."

Lynn looked down at her feet.

I was pretty sure Charlotte was trying to get rid of me. And I thought I knew why. Charlotte was mad at me. She liked being the best dancer in class. I had outdone her that day.

"It was no big deal, Charlotte," I said. "You don't have to be jealous."

"Jealous?" Charlotte repeated. "Why would I be jealous?"

"Because my *royales* are better than yours," I told her.

Charlotte laughed. "Oh, that! Pat was just being nice to you because you're new."

I stomped my foot. "That's not true!" I yelled.

Mr. Stein poked his head out of the studio where his class was going on. "Could you girls please keep it down?" he asked. "We can't hear the music in here. Charlotte Stype, I'm surprised at you."

"It wasn't me," Charlotte said. She nodded in my direction. "Becky is being a crybaby."

"Well, whatever is going on, keep it down," Mr. Stein said. He disappeared back into the studio.

At that moment I hated Charlotte more than I ever hated anyone. She had made Katie mad at me and she had insulted my dancing *twice*.

I pushed past Charlotte and Lynn, ran down the stairs, and stormed out of the building. I didn't care that I was still wearing my leotard, tights, and slippers. Outside I stopped to put on my jacket. I took a few shaky deep breaths. That was to stop me from crying.

I knew Charlotte and Lynn would come out at any second. I didn't want them to see me, so I hurried toward home. As I passed the coffee shop, I caught a glimpse of my friends inside. They were sitting at our favorite booth, spying on people walking down the street, like we always do.

Katie caught my eye. I could tell she was surprised to see me alone and in my ballet clothes. I ducked my head so Katie wouldn't see how upset I was.

I started running and kept running until I got to my room. I closed the door and locked it. I could hear Angela playing a game with Lena in the kitchen. Sophie and one of her friends were giggling in her room.

I put my face into my pillow and cried.

I had never felt more alone.

Sixteen

Baby Blue

"Yuck," I moaned when I woke up on Thursday. It was cold and drizzling. The sky was gray. Just looking out the window made my head hurt and my stomach ache. I decided I was too sick to go to school. I pulled the covers up to my chin.

It was a relief to be sick. I was dreading ballet class that afternoon.

I squeezed my eyes shut and flopped from side to side. I couldn't get back to sleep. I kept thinking about Charlotte and Katie.

I knew I owed Katie an apology. I had more or less ignored her ever since Charlotte had started paying attention to me. I couldn't believe how awful I had been about the party. Totally uncool.

I rolled over on my back and let out a loud sigh. I felt grumpy. I hate to say I'm sorry. I wasn't looking forward to apologizing to Katie. I didn't even know if Katie would listen. She had tried to say sorry to me, and I hadn't listened to *her*.

Charlotte was a different story. I thought she owed *me* an apology. She had lied to Katie; she had lied about her parents' dinner party, and she had been mean about my *royales*. Come to think of it, she owed me three apologies.

Ballet that afternoon was definitely going to be a mess.

I pulled the covers over my head.

"Wake up, Becky!" Sophie yelled into my room. "Mom has breakfast ready. And it's your day to make Lena's lunch."

"Leave me alone," I said. "I'm sick."

"Faker," Sophie said, but she went to the top of the stairs and yelled down to Mom. "Becky says she's sick!"

Lena came into my room a few minutes later. She crawled onto my bed and pulled the covers down around my toes.

"Good morning!" Lena yelled.

"Cut it out," I growled, pulling the covers back up.

"Mom said you have to get out of bed," Lena announced. "Get up!"

"I can't," I told her. "I'm too weak from fever."

Lena hopped out of my bed and put her hand on my forehead. She pursed her lips just like Mom does when she's testing to see if one of us kids has a fever.

"No fever," Lena announced. "Cool as a cucumber. Get up, get up, get up!" She pulled the covers off me again.

"That isn't funny," I told Lena. But I crawled out of bed. When my little sister wants you up, you get up. It's pointless to resist. That's why Mom sent her in to get me.

"I'm out of bed," I told Lena. "Now, get lost or else I'll make you a prune sandwich for lunch."

Lena ran out of the room. "I want peanut butter and honey," she said from the doorway. "No prunes. They make you—"

"I know!" I yelled. "I know."

Lena skipped into the hallway. "Becky's up!" I heard her yell downstairs to Mom.

I stomped down the hall to the bathroom. I brushed my teeth and washed my face as slowly as possible. Then I stomped back to my room and started looking for something to wear.

I found a sweatshirt and a pair of jeans on the closet floor. They were clean except for a few spots.

Then I remembered I needed my ballet clothes. My drawers were empty. I got down on my hands and knees and looked under the bed. My pink leotard and both pairs of my tights were under there. They were rolled together in a little ball. Naturally, they were dirty. In fact, they smelled like old gym shoes.

I know what you're thinking. I admit it. I'm not the neatest person in the world. On my last birthday Katie gave me a sign for my bedroom door: BECKY'S JUNKYARD. I can't help it if I'm messy. I have better things to do in life than fold clothes.

"Good morning, pumpkin," Mom said when I got downstairs. "I'm glad you're feeling better."

"Mom," I whined. "My pink leotard and tights are dirty."

"I did all the laundry in the hamper," Mom said. "Where were they?"

"Under my bed," I admitted.

Mom shook her head. "Well, find something else to wear. And hurry. You have about ten minutes before you have to leave for school."

I stomped up the stairs.

"Don't forget Lena's lunch," Mom yelled after me. "She wants a peanut-butter-and-honey sandwich."

"I know!" I yelled as loudly as I could.

I stuffed an old blue leotard and my least dirty pair of tights (yuck!) into my bag. I didn't have a choice. I knew Pat wouldn't mind if I wore the wrong-color leotard, but it made me feel like a baby.

It was going to be a terrible day. I could just feel it.

Seventeen

Charlotte's Grudge

I like to run to ballet class. By the time school is over, I'm usually too excited to walk. The whole time I've been a pink, I haven't waited for Megan and Nikki even once. They take too long.

But that afternoon, when the last bell rang, I got out of my seat slowly. I stopped to ask Mr. Cosgrove about our homework assignment. I started to put my books away in my locker. Then I decided to arrange them in alphabetical order. Before I could do that, I had to clean out all the candy wrappers and balled-up homework assignments. (My locker isn't much neater than my room.)

I was kneeling down by my locker when Hillary Widmer stopped next to me. She was wearing sweatpants and a sweatshirt. She was carrying a softball and glove.

"Want to come play softball?" Hillary asked me. "We need another player."

I was tempted, but I shook my head. "I have ballet today," I told Hillary.

"Why don't you skip it?" Hillary asked.

I thought about that. "I'd better not," I finally said. "Have a good game."

"We will!" Hillary said. She ran down the hall.

I got up and *walked* toward the ballet school. I walked as slowly as possible. On the way I looked in all the windows on Main Street, even the library and hardware-store windows.

By the time I got to the dressing room, only Nikki was still there. Her hair was already up in a bun.

"Hi!" Nikki greeted me. "Did you just get here? I thought you were already in the studio. Class starts in about two minutes."

"I know," I said.

"You'd better hurry," Nikki told me. She pushed open the door and rushed out.

I changed and dragged myself into the studio.

Al was already seated at the piano.

Pat was taking attendance.

I looked around. The only spot left was in the corner of the room, behind Kim.

"Becky, hurry up and get settled," Pat said. She looked surprised by my blue leotard but didn't say anything. "I'm ready to start."

I ran over and took the place behind Kim.

Megan, Nikki, and Risa each turned around and smiled at me. I tried to catch Katie's eye, but she ignored me. I was getting worried. Apologizing to Katie was going to be even harder than I thought. What if she really didn't want to be my friend anymore? What if she said sorry wasn't good enough?

Pat started the barre. I knew the exercises by heart. But I was worried about Katie, and I couldn't concentrate on them.

"Becky," Pat said. "These are *demi-pliés,* not *grand pliés.*"

"Sorry," I said.

"Becky, watch out," Kim whispered to me. "You hit me with your hand three times already."

"Sorry," I said.

"Becky," Pat said. "Arms to the side."

"Sorry," I said.

The rest of the barre was like that. I was a mess.

"Let's move into the center," Pat said finally. "Becky, try and wake up, okay?"

"I'll try," I said. I took my usual position next to Charlotte.

"Hi," I whispered to her.

Charlotte did not answer. She didn't even glance at me. That made me mad. I understood

115

why Katie was acting like I was invisible. But I could not believe Charlotte was still mad at me. All I had done was say her *royales* weren't perfect.

I was busy being mad at Charlotte, so I couldn't concentrate on the center work. When the others bent down, I jumped up. When the others raised their right arms, I raised my left.

"Maybe you should go back to the beginners' class," Charlotte whispered to me. "You already look like a baby in that blue leotard."

I felt tears well up in my eyes, but I blinked them back.

While everyone else was concentrating on their traveling steps, I thought about what Katie had said when we had our fight. She had said Charlotte only liked me because I kept telling her that she was a great dancer.

I thought back on my afternoons in Charlotte's studio. I tried to count up how many times I said Charlotte was terrific. I couldn't count that high.

Charlotte had been acting like she was my best friend. But as soon as I noticed she wasn't perfect, Charlotte wouldn't even talk to me.

Could Katie have been right? I shook my head. I couldn't believe it. I still thought Charlotte and I were friends.

Eighteen

Jumps and Giggles

"I'm going to teach you a new jump," Pat told us just before the end of class. "It's called a *pas de chat*. The name is French for 'step of the cat.' You'll like it. It's fun to do."

Pat demonstrated the step. I could see where its name came from. The jump looked a lot like a cat pouncing on a mouse.

"You start in fifth position with your left foot in front," Pat explained. "Do a *demi-plié*. Jump to the right keeping the toes of your right leg level with your left knee. Then raise your left leg to the same position as your right. Turn your head to the right. Land in a *demi-plié* in fifth position with your left foot in front."

Pat did several more *pas de chats*.

I shook my head. The jumps looked hard.

All around me other kids were whispering

about the jump. Nobody said anything to me. It was as if the whole world were mad at me. I knew that wasn't true. Risa and Nikki and Megan were being careful not to choose sides in my fight with Katie. But that did not stop me from feeling alone.

"Okay," Pat said. "Let's try it."

Everyone lined up. This time I took a place in the back, between Kim and Philip. We stepped into fifth position.

Al began playing.

"One, two, three, four," Pat counted. "And— *plié*, jump, lift your leg, and land."

I didn't get any further than the second count. When we were supposed to jump to the right, I jumped to the left. Kim jumped to the right, just like she was supposed to. We crashed into each other and landed in a heap on the floor.

"I'm sorry," I told Kim. I stood up and reached a hand down toward her.

Kim giggled as she got back on her feet. "Don't worry," she said. "That was kind of fun."

Kim and I weren't the only ones to end up on the floor. The *pas de chats* were even harder than they looked. Lots of other kids in the class bumped into each other and crashed. Some just fell over all by themselves.

Al shook his head in disgust.

118

"Very good!" Pat yelled.

Everyone cracked up at that.

Just then Madame Trikilnova swept into the studio.

Everyone stopped laughing.

"Ms. Kelly," Madame Trikilnova said. "What is the meaning of all of this noise?"

Pat smiled. "The class was just trying a few *pas de chats*. Charlotte, why don't you come up front and show Madame Trikilnova what we've been working on."

Charlotte stepped to the front.

Madame Trikilnova raised her eyebrows and frowned at Charlotte.

Charlotte smiled back at her. She didn't look one bit nervous.

I bit my lip, wondering what was going to happen. I knew how much Charlotte admired Madame Trikilnova. Was she about to look stupid in front of her?

Al began to play.

Charlotte did six *pas de chats* across the front of the room. They were perfect.

"Lovely," Madame Trikilnova told Charlotte. She nodded at Pat and swept out the door.

Everyone let out a sigh of relief.

"That's it, gang," Pat announced. We broke into applause. "See you on Tuesday."

I forgot I was supposed to be mad at Charlotte. I hurried up to her.

"You were great," I said. "Madame Trikilnova really looked impressed!"

"I know," Charlotte said. "But don't expect me to teach you that jump. I'm not spending any more of my time with a baby beginner."

My jaw dropped. "I thought we were friends," I said.

Charlotte sneered at me. "You're not good enough to be my friend."

Nineteen

Katie to the Rescue

Hot tears rose up in my eyes. Without seeing where I was going, I ran out into the hallway. The tears welled over and streamed down my face.

Katie had been right all along.

Charlotte had never been my friend. Charlotte didn't want friends. She wanted fans.

"Becky? Are you all right?"

I sniffled and looked up.

Katie was standing in front of me. She looked worried. Megan, Risa, and Nikki were right behind her. They looked worried, too.

"I'm—I'm okay," I managed to say. It's hard to talk when you're crying hard.

Katie put her arm around my shoulders. "What happened?"

"Charlotte," I choked out. "Charlotte said—" I had to stop and take a deep breath.

"Who cares what Charlotte said?" Katie asked. "Don't pay any attention to her. She's just jealous because you're such a good dancer."

I looked up.

Megan, Risa, and Nikki were all nodding.

I couldn't believe they thought I was a good dancer. It made me feel a little better.

"How come you're being so nice to me?" I asked Katie.

"Because you're my best friend," Katie answered.

"She's been miserable without you," Risa said.

"No joke," Nikki added.

Katie rolled her eyes, but then she smiled. "I did miss you," she admitted.

"I thought you were mad at me," I told Katie.

"I am—I *was* a little mad," Katie admitted. "I couldn't believe you went to Charlotte's on the day of the party."

"I waited—" I started to explain.

Katie waved her hands wildly. "Shhh!"

Risa, Megan, and Nikki fell silent. They were staring down the hall. I turned to see what they were looking at.

A tall, thin boy with wavy dark hair and big green eyes had just come out of the advanced class. He walked down the hall toward the stairs.

As he passed, he looked right at me and frowned at my tear-stained face.

"Cheer up," he told me. Then he disappeared into the stairwell.

Megan clasped her hand over her heart. Nikki slumped against the wall. Katie and Risa sighed.

"That was him, wasn't it?" I asked. "That was Chris Adabo!"

"Definitely," Risa said.

"Isn't he adorable?" Katie asked.

"Totally," I said.

"I can't believe he talked to you," Megan squealed.

I shook my head. "Me either!"

Just then Pat came out of the studio. She frowned at the five of us standing in the hallway.

"Is everything okay, you guys?" Pat asked.

"Everything's great," Katie told her.

"Just great," I seconded.

It felt wonderful to be back with my real friends again.

Twenty

Old Friends

"Hi!" Dean yelled as Katie, Megan, Risa, Nikki, and I walked into the coffee shop. He and Philip were stacking dishes behind the counter.

"Hi!" we yelled back.

Risa ran ahead to our favorite booth and grabbed one of the window seats. The rest of us joined her.

Dean came over to our table, carrying a pad and pencil. I guessed his father hadn't taught him how to memorize orders.

"What do you guys want?" Dean asked.

"A hot-fudge sundae," Nikki announced, "with Double Chocolate Chip ice cream."

Megan made an awful face. "Nikki, that's so gross," she said. "You're going to die of a chocolate overdose."

"Sounds like a great way to go," Nikki said.

125

Megan rolled her eyes. "I'd like a hot-fudge sundae with vanilla ice cream," she told Dean.

"That's my favorite," Dean told her.

"Butterscotch sundae on Fudge Ripple," Risa ordered.

"Hot fudge on Peppermint Stick," Katie said.

"I'll just have water," I said.

All of my friends turned to stare at me. Dean stared, too.

"What's the deal?" Katie asked.

"I haven't gotten my allowance yet," I explained.

Katie opened her wallet and poured a pile of change on the table. She counted it up. "Order a sundae," she told me. "I'll loan you the money."

"Thanks, Katie," I said. "I'll have hot fudge on Double Chocolate Chip ice cream," I told Dean.

"Good choice!" Nikki said.

Megan rolled her eyes.

Dean laughed and walked back behind the counter.

"Did you guys see Madame Trikilnova today?" Megan asked.

"How could we miss her?" I asked. "She scared me to death."

"I was afraid I was going to laugh when she came into the studio," Megan said.

"How come?" I asked.

126

Megan giggled. "She was covered in cat hair!" she said.

Risa shook her head. "Madame Trikilnova loves Giselle."

"And Giselle's hairs love Madame Trikilnova's black leotards," Katie added.

Risa turned to watch Jillian Kormach walk by outside.

"Jillian almost fell on her face today in class," she commented.

"I can't believe she doesn't dance better," Megan said.

Risa wrinkled her nose. "I don't like Jillian much."

"Why not?" I asked.

"She's snobby," Nikki said. "All she talks about is living in New York City and going to her fancy ballet school."

"She's a big bragger," Risa agreed.

"I bet she thinks she's better than us small-town kids," Katie added.

"I guess—" Megan said. "But it's hard to be new. I kind of feel sorry for her."

Dean came back with the ice cream. "I made these myself," he announced.

He placed a sundae in front of each of us and marched proudly away with his empty tray.

Katie looked down at the table and raised her eyebrows.

Four of our sundaes were normal size. Megan's was extra big.

I gave Megan a funny look.

Megan pretended not to notice anything unusual, but she was blushing.

I wondered if Dean liked Megan. And did Megan like him?

While I was thinking about that and taking a huge bite of my sundae, Charlotte and Lynn walked by. Lynn waved at us, but Charlotte walked by without looking in.

I felt angry at Charlotte all over again. I couldn't believe I had expected her to say she was sorry. Charlotte is too proud to ever admit she did something wrong.

"What happened with Charlotte today?" Katie asked me. "You don't have to tell us if you don't want to," she added quickly.

"She said I wasn't good enough to be her friend," I whispered.

"No way!" Nikki exclaimed.

"That's silly," Megan said. "You guys are already friends."

I shook my head. "I think Charlotte only liked me because I said nice things about her dancing."

Risa and Megan nodded.

"Charlotte is totally stuck on herself," Nikki commented.

Katie didn't say anything. Not even "I told you so."

My friends would never understand, but at that moment I decided I would like to be friends with Charlotte again someday. Of course, she would have to apologize first.

Do you think I'm crazy? Well, think about this. Charlotte is the only person I have ever met who loves ballet as much as I do. How could I help but want to be friends with her?

"Hey, Katie," I said instead of sharing my thoughts about Charlotte. "I've been meaning to ask you. What's the deal with Al? Dean says he's strange."

"Sometimes he is," Katie said.

"Do you mean like when he rolls his eyes at us in class?" I asked.

"No," Katie said. "I mean like the time he wore a hat to class."

"What's so strange about that?" I asked.

Risa giggled. "It was one of those hats with a spinner on top," she explained.

"Once he played standing up for an entire class," Megan added. "We never found out why."

"One time Pat asked him to play a certain

song," Nikki said. "And he wouldn't. He said it made him sad."

I shook my head. "I think you guys are making this stuff up. Al always acts normal when I'm around. Well, almost always."

"You saw him do something, didn't you?" Nikki asked me.

"No," I said. "But . . ."

"But what?" Nikki prompted.

"It was on the first day of class," I said. "After everyone else was gone, he came up to me and said, 'You will make it!'"

"What does that mean?" Risa asked.

"Beats me," I said.

Katie shook her head. "It's obvious," she said. "He meant you'll make it as a ballerina. I think Al was right."

I stared at Katie. She had never encouraged me like that before. I was shocked.

Just then Nikki's mom appeared on the street, outside our booth. She peered inside. When she spotted Nikki, she knocked on the glass and motioned for her to come out.

Nikki groaned. "I guess I have to go." She threw her money down and hurried outside.

"Bye, Nikki," we all called.

Our sundaes were gone. It was time for all of us

to go. We paid, and even left Dean a quarter tip.

Katie and I said good-bye to Risa and Megan outside the coffee shop. As Katie and I headed home, I told her I was sorry about everything that had happened.

"It's okay," Katie said. "I'm sorry, too. I shouldn't have yelled at you. You were right. I *was* a little jealous of you and Charlotte."

"You didn't need to be jealous," I told her. "Charlotte could never take your place."

"Why not?" Katie asked.

"For one thing, she wasn't around to protect me from Max," I said.

"The boy who sat behind you in first grade?" Katie asked.

I nodded. "He was such a bully!" I said. "He stole my milk money every day. I was terrified of him."

"He didn't scare me," Katie said proudly. "*I* scared *him*."

"What did you tell him that made him leave me alone?" I asked.

"I said I was a witch," Katie explained. "I told him that if he didn't leave you alone, I would cast a spell on him. I said I would turn him into a *girl*!"

"You saved my life," I told her with a laugh.

"I owed you," Katie said. "You protected me from the mean dog on Cedar Street."

131

"You mean the poodle?" I asked.

We both cracked up.

After a moment I took a deep breath. "How was the party?" I asked carefully.

Katie groaned. "How do you think it was?" she asked.

"I think it was awful," I said.

"It was worse than awful," Katie said. "It was *horrendous*. Nikki tried to cheer me up, but there was no way."

"I'm sorry," I whispered.

"Don't worry about it," Katie said. "You've done worse things to me."

"Like what?" I demanded.

"Like the time you threw my doll into the ocean," Katie said.

"Katie!" I exclaimed. "That was years ago."

"It was my favorite doll," Katie said.

"Well, I'm sorry I drowned it," I told her.

"I should get over it by the time I'm fifty," Katie said.

"Do you think we'll still be friends then?" I asked.

"Definitely," Katie said.

We walked along without talking for a minute, each thinking our own thoughts.

"I want to ask you something," Katie said.

"What?" I asked.

132

"How did Charlotte pull off those *pas de chats* in front of Madame Trikilnova?" Katie asked.

"She must have learned the jump ahead of time," I explained. "Charlotte has a big ballet book at home. It has illustrations that show you how to do different steps. She sometimes practices things we haven't learned in class."

"Can you do a *pas de chat*?" Katie asked.

"Maybe with a little practice," I said. "Come on!"

Katie and I joined hands. We practiced our *pas de chats* down the sidewalk. By the time we got to Katie's house, we had them down.

"I can't wait for class on Tuesday," I said. "Pat is going to be so impressed with us."

"Should I save you a place at the barre?" Katie asked.

I smiled. "Of course," I said. "I wouldn't stand anywhere but next to my best friend."

Don't miss **JILLIAN ON HER TOES,** *the next book in this great new series!*

Arabesque en pointe

The Five Basic Positions

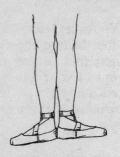

First position

Second position

Third position

Fourth position

Fifth position

WHAT THE BALLET WORDS MEAN

Battement frappé (bat-MAHN fra-PAY) An exercise. To do it, cross the heel of your right foot behind the ankle of your left foot. Point your right foot to the side. Then cross your right heel in front of your left ankle. This exercise is usually repeated many times. You can also try switching feet. Two or more of these movements are called *battements frappés*.

Changement (shahnzh-MAHN) A move in which you jump up with one leg in front and land with the other leg in front. Two or more are called *changements*.

Demi-plié (de-MEE plee-AY) A half knee-bend.

En pointe (ahn pwahnt) Dancing *en pointe* or "on pointe" means dancing on your toes. Ballet dancers use special shoes to dance *en pointe*. Girls start dancing on their toes when they are about twelve. Before then, their bones are too soft.

Jeté (je-TAY) A type of jump. In a *grand jeté* the dancer opens her arms and legs wide.

Pas de bourrée (pah duh boo-RAY) A traveling step.

Pas de chat (pah duh shah) means "step of the cat" in French. It's a traveling step that looks a lot like a cat pouncing on a mouse.

Pirouette (peer-oo-ET) is French for "whirl." It's a kind of turn in which the dancer spins around on one foot.

Plié (plee-AY) is a knee bend.

Positions Almost every step in ballet begins and ends with the dancer's feet in one of five positions. The positions are called first, second, third, fourth, and fifth. The drawing on p. 135 shows the positions. Some ballet instructors use French words to describe the positions: *première, seconde, troisième, quatrième,* and *cinquième.*

Relevé (ruhluh-VAY) An exercise in which you rise up on the balls of your feet.

Rosin A white powder that dancers rub into the soles of their shoes to stop them from slipping.

Royale (roh-YAL) A type of *changement.* In a *royale,* a dancer hits her calves together before changing the position of her feet.

Spotting A technique dancers use to keep them from getting dizzy when they turn.

Toe shoes Special shoes dancers wear to rise up on their toes. The toe area of the shoe is hard. Also called *pointe* shoes.

Turnout Dancers turn their legs out to the sides from their hips to help them lift their legs higher. This is called turnout.

Tutu (tew-TEW) A very short skirt worn by a ballet dancer.

ABOUT THE AUTHOR

Emily Costello was born in Cincinnati, Ohio, and now lives in New York City. She likes to eat spaghetti, play tennis, and see movies. She has two left feet but enjoys watching ballet.